MERRY

A NOVELLA

MARY

ASHLEY FARLEY

For all my angels

ALSO BY ASHLEY FARLEY

Magnolia Nights

Sweet Tea Tuesdays

Saving Ben

Sweeney Sisters Series

Saturdays at Sweeney's

Tangle of Strings

Boots and Bedlam

Lowcountry Stranger

Her Sister's Shoes

Adventures of Scottie

Breaking the Story

1

The first rays of pink sunshine ushered in another day of suffering for the people who called Monroe Park in downtown Richmond home. An early winter storm had dumped six inches of snow on the city. With no clouds to blanket in warmth, temperatures had dipped into the teens for the third night in a row.

Scottie Darden parked her 4Runner alongside the dirty snowbanks on Main Street. She pulled her stocking cap down over her blonde mane and tucked her camera inside her down coat. Grabbing the two Bojangles' bags and carton of coffee from the backseat, she trudged through the snow to a cluster of men and women huddled around a burning trash can.

Eyeing the bags of food, the group of five homeless people navigated toward Scottie. She handed out sausage biscuits and paper cups of coffee.

Scottie had stumbled upon the Five by accident a year ago while investigating a series of muggings in the area. Their despondent faces had such a profound impact on Scottie that she'd returned the next day with warm blankets and buckets of fried chicken from Lee's. Their gratitude had moved her even more, and over the next twelve months, she'd stopped by on a regular basis, always delivering nourishment and supplies. She'd seen others come and go, but this core group of five banded together like a family.

"I brought extras today." Scottie held up the second bag.

Mabel gestured toward a row of makeshift tents fifty feet in front of them. Her name wasn't really Mabel. At least not as far as Scottie knew. With gray hair pulled back from her café au lait face, the old woman reminded Scottie of the housekeeper who once worked for her grandmother.

Scottie had never exchanged names with any of the Five. She'd grown to know them by their physical appearances instead.

Buck was a strapping black man of about thirty, the one Scottie feared the most because of the temper she sensed smoldering just beneath the surface Then there was Pops, the oldest male, with leathery skin the color of dark chocolate. While he never showed his teeth, Scottie often detected the hint of a smile tugging along his lips. She'd named the woman with the plain face and dull green eyes Miss Cecil after her third grade teacher. She referred to the man in the wheelchair, with both legs amputated at the knee, as Dan, after Lieutenant Dan in the movie *Forrest Gump*.

Scottie offered each of the Five another biscuit before moving to the makeshift tents. She passed out biscuits to women and men who were buried under blankets and sleeping bags. She heard the faint sound of crying outside the fourth tent. She tapped lightly on the cardboard door. When no one responded and the crying grew louder, she pulled back the cardboard and peeked inside.

"Hello in there," she called in a soft voice. "Can I interest you in some breakfast?"

The crying intensified to a squall. Beneath a threadbare blanket, Scottie made out the unmoving form of an adult-size body and the flailing limbs of a smaller figure next to it.

"Hello." Scottie dropped to her knees and crawled inside. "Can I hold your baby for you while you eat a biscuit?"

When the adult body remained still, Scottie peeled back the blankets to reveal a baby—three or four months old if she had to guess—with blonde peach fuzz on top of her head and a beet-red face. A girl, judging from the dirty pink fleece sleeper she was wearing. She pulled the covers back the rest of the way and gasped at the sight of the woman's gray skin and purple lips. Scottie assumed the woman was the baby's mother. She backed slowly out of the tent. "Someone, please help!" she cried. "I think this woman in here is dead."

The Five fled the scene, along with every other homeless man and woman in sight. Scottie patted her pockets for her phone, then remembered she'd left it connected to the charger on her bedside table. She surveyed the area for help—a policeman, a student, a businessman on his way to work—but the park was deserted.

Scottie crawled back inside and picked up the baby, rocking her back and forth until she settled down a bit. She scooted over closer to the baby's mother and checked her wrist and neck for a pulse, but there was none. The woman had been dead long enough for her skin to grow cold. Her eyes were closed, but her rosy lips were turned up into a smile, as though she'd seen an angel. Poor woman was probably no more than twenty years old.

Scottie pulled the blanket over the woman's face and said a silent prayer.

Getting to a phone to call for help was the only thing on her mind when she zipped the baby inside her coat and made a dash for her car.

2

S cottie lay the baby in the passenger seat next to her. She started the engine and cranked up the heat. With one hand resting on the baby's chest, she navigated the back streets of the Fan toward home. She had driven several blocks before her heart rate slowed and she began to process the situation. The medical examiner would take possession of the young mother's body to await identification by the next of kin. *If* there even *was* a next of kin. The woman had been living on the streets. Where was her family? And what about the baby's father? The makeshift tent they'd been sleeping in was tiny, too small for another body.

Then there was the matter of an autopsy. Scottie assumed the mother had died of hypothermia, but what if that wasn't the case? What if the young woman had overdosed on drugs, or worse, if her scorned lover had murdered her during the night? Scottie hadn't seen any blood, at least not in the upper region of the body, but that's not to say she hadn't been stabbed in the gut. Scottie's mind raced. If the woman had in fact been murdered, she had not only tampered with evidence at the scene of a crime, she had wrongfully taken the child away from the scene.

She pulled up in front of her row house on West Avenue and put the SUV in gear. She beat the steering wheel with the palm of her hand. "God, Scottie, how could you be so stupid?" she said in a voice loud enough to make the baby cry.

"Shh, don't cry," she said, rubbing the baby's tummy.

What would become of the baby? Scottie didn't think the Commonwealth had the authority to place the baby up for adoption without permission of next of kin, which meant the baby would be placed in a foster home until the police could track down the father. *If* the father even wanted the child. *If* the father even knew he was the father.

The baby began to wail, presumably with hunger. "Don't worry, little one." She picked the baby up and held her tight. "We'll get it all sorted out. In the meantime, I have plenty of formula and diapers to keep you comfortable."

By the time Scottie got the baby inside, and mixed up a bottle from the supplies in her baby cabinet in the kitchen, the little girl was screaming, flailing her arms and legs in hunger. Scottie plopped down on the leather sofa in the adjoining family room, propped her snow boots up on the coffee table, and brought the bottle's nipple to the baby's mouth. The infant took the nipple between her lips, then thrust it back out with her tongue. Scottie turned the bottle upside down on her arm, letting a few drops of formula leak from the hole in the nipple, before returning the nipple to the baby's lips. When she tasted the formula, the baby began to suck greedily.

"Careful now, baby girl. Don't drink too fast or you'll upset your tummy." The baby stared up at Scottie with bright eyes. "We need to give you a name, don't we?"

Scottie had been in the process of picking out names for her baby when her daughter was stillborn at thirty-one weeks. She'd been torn between Kate and Liza, after her grandmothers Katherine and Elizabeth. She ended up calling the baby Angel, which seemed appropriate for an innocent child who never drew her first breath.

Scottie's eyes traveled the room, coming to rest on the nativity scene on the mantle above the fireplace. "Why don't we call you Mary after the Virgin Mary?" She caught sight of the needlepoint pillow Brad had brought down from the attic—a green background with *Merry Christmas* in curlicue script in red across the front. "Or Merry, which seems appropriate for a spunky little girl like you."

The baby stopped sucking and smiled up at her.

"I agree," Scottie said. "I like them both as well. Merry Mary it is, then."

Scottie drew in a deep breath and sank further into the sofa. Exhausted already and it was only eleven o'clock in the morning. She reached for the remote control and powered on the television, tuning in to the local ABC affiliate. The cast of *The View* was seated around a table discussing the day's news. Scottie was certain a unit had been dispatched to the park by now, although the discovery of a dead homeless person was rarely considered breaking news.

She wondered how long it would take the police to learn of the missing baby.

Scottie thought of her cell phone charging on the bedside table upstairs. As soon as Mary finished her bottle, she would call the police and explain the situation. No harm would be done, and they'd whisk the baby off to a foster home where she'd spend the rest of her life neglected and abused.

"That's settled, then, Merry Mary. I don't see any harm in providing you with a warm place to stay and all the formula you can eat. At least not until the authorities locate your family."

Scottie removed the bottle from Mary's mouth and lifted the baby to the burp cloth on her shoulder, rubbing her back until she let out a loud burp.

"That's a good girl. I bet you feel better now." She returned the baby to the crook of her arm and gave her back the bottle.

Scottie watched Mary's eyes dart around the room, from the table lamp beside them to the canned light in the ceiling to the Christmas tree in the corner. Brad had dragged the tree home a week ago and strung it with lights, but so far, Scottie lacked the motivation to hang the ornaments. She wasn't in the mood for celebrating the holidays this year.

Following the loss of her baby in March, Scottie's father suffered a near-fatal heart attack and subsequent quadruple bypass in April. Even her job as a freelance photojournalist, which had always inspired her, had begun to dishearten her lately with the constant arguing between the political parties in Washington and the endless mass shootings. Terrorist groups like ISIS and Al-Qaeda remained a threat, but Americans killing Americans en masse on American soil was even more heartbreaking to Scottie.

The faces of the Five stared down at her from various positions on the wall. Brad had been after her to take down the framed photographs for some time. "All these sad and lonely people are depressing me," he'd said.

Scottie visited the Five a half dozen times before she dared to bring out her camera. They didn't mind if she took their picture as long as she handed out hot food in exchange. The emotions she captured were genuine and raw—anger and pain, loneliness and helplessness. She called her collection the *Lost Souls*. Two or three more photographs and she'd have enough for a gallery showing.

The baby sucked the remaining formula out of the bottle and let out a contented burp. "Good gracious! Most men don't burp that loud."

Mary tensed her body and scrunched up her face, grunting as she pooped.

"I bet it's been a while since anyone changed your diaper,"

she said and clucked her tongue at the baby. "But that's all right. We'll get you cleaned up in no time."

Scottie carried the baby up the steep flight of stairs to the second floor. After her first pregnancy ended in miscarriage, she'd been cautiously optimistic when she made it through the first trimester the second time around. Even more so when her midpregnancy ultrasound revealed a completely formed fetus. Confident she would deliver a healthy baby, her friends had thrown her a big shower and outfitted her nursery with all the high-tech baby products on today's market. And Scottie had spent hours watching YouTube videos on every infant care subject available—from breastfeeding to bathing to bedtime routines.

She laid Mary on the changing table and stripped off her filthy sleeper and rancid diaper, gasping at the sight of the infant's body. Dirt was caked in the creases of her skin and a rash covered her neck and bottom.

With the naked baby tucked under one arm, Scottie gathered the things she needed for her bath and headed down the hall to the bathroom.

She filled the infant tub and lowered the baby into the warm water. Mary splashed and kicked the water with delight. "Looks like Merry Mary likes her bath," Scottie cooed. She lathered the baby with soap, then rinsed away the dirt with a soft washcloth. She lifted her out of the tub, dried her thoroughly, and wrapped her in a hooded towel for the trip back to the nursery. After coating Mary's bottom in Desitin cream, she squeezed her into a newborn-size diaper, and maneuvered her little limbs into the largest sleeper she could find.

"First chance we get, we'll go shopping for supplies."

Once in her crib, Mary fell asleep before Scottie could close the blinds and turn off the light.

Scottie stretched out on the twin bed beside the crib. *No wonder my friends with babies are always complaining about being tired,* she thought before drifting off to sleep.

3

The ringing of the doorbell followed by the loud tapping of the brass knocker woke Scottie an hour later. *Mother.* Only Barbara Westport announced her arrival with such enthusiasm. Scottie hopped to her feet and tiptoed out of the nursery. She was halfway down the stairs when the bell rang again.

Scottie swung the front door open. "Geez, Mom. Give the doorbell a rest. I heard you the first time."

Her mother eyed Scottie's disheveled appearance. "Time to get up, sweetheart. I thought you'd given up sleeping until noon in college." Barbara brushed past her in a cloud of Chanel No. 5 perfume.

"For your information, I was taking a nap." Scottie followed her mother through the house to the back room. "I got up at the crack of dawn to work this morning."

Barbara stopped in front of her bare Christmas tree. "And just what have you been working on? Obviously not your tree."

Scottie's parents lived on a spread of land in Goochland, twenty minutes west of Richmond toward Charlottesville. Every year, on the day after Thanksgiving, her mother decked their

Dutch Colonial farmhouse out in bows of holly and every other kind of evergreen that grew on their property.

Aside from her L.L. Bean gumshoes, Barbara appeared the picture of elegance dressed in gray flannel slacks, a gray cashmere sweater, and a lavender wool cape. Her dark hair and eyes were in stark contrast to her daughter's. Scottie took after her father's Swedish ancestors, while her brother, Will, was the spitting image of their mother.

"I plan to finish the tree today, Mom. I've been working on my series."

Her mother shot a glance at the *Lost Soul* photograph nearest her. "Please tell me you haven't been in the slums taking pictures of those filthy vagrants again."

Barbara was no stranger to volunteer work. She frequented soup kitchens and raised money for a number of different charities. One year she served as Christmas Mother for the *Times-Dispatch* Christmas Mother Fund, a program that raised funds to provide toys, clothing, food, and other assistance to needy families and children across the area.

"I was delivering hot food to the homeless. I don't see how that's any different than working in a soup kitchen."

"There's a big difference, Scottie, and you know it. You won't catch me venturing into unsafe neighborhoods." Barbara wagged her finger at Scottie. "And you shouldn't either. Your husband and I don't see eye to eye on much, but his concern about the safety of your . . . hobby is one thing we have in common."

Scottie's parents had warned her against marrying Brad. They'd not only been concerned about their daughter getting married right out of college, they'd also seen straight through Brad's big talk.

"Don't be so quick to believe everything he says, honey," her mother had warned, while her father had suggested they wait a year or two until they got to know each other better. When all their attempts to persuade Scottie to postpone the marriage failed, her mother had even begged them to try living together first, a proposal that contradicted her parents' traditional values.

"I'm thirty-years old, Mom. I can take care of myself."

"I'm not so sure about that, if the state of your home is any indication." Barbara noticed the nativity scene above the fireplace. "At least you decorated your mantle."

"Ha. I never took it down from last year."

"Well, then." Barbara dropped her Stella McCartney hobo bag on the sofa. "Lucky for you I'm free this afternoon. We can have this tree decorated in no time."

Scottie picked up the purse and handed it back to her mother. "Thanks, Mom, but I can handle the tree myself. I'll probably wait until Brad gets home, anyway."

Her mother arched a manicured eyebrow. "I didn't realize Brad was away."

"He's gone to California for his annual Christmas visit with his family."

"Ah, yes, the Phantom Fam."

Scottie hated it when her mother threw her own words back in her face. Brad's family wasn't exactly a figment of their imaginations. They'd all met his obnoxious, opinionated parents when they came for their wedding seven years ago. They'd just never returned to Virginia again. Never mind that he never asked Scottie to go to California with him. The one time she'd confronted him about it, he'd made a lame excuse about being unable to afford the airfare.

"Back off, Mom. Just because we live in the same city doesn't mean I have to report every detail of my life to you."

"You're right. Sorry. I was out of line." Barbara hoisted her bag onto her shoulder. "At least let me run out and grab a wreath for your front door and a poinsettia for your table."

"No, really, Mom, you don't need to worry. It won't be the end of the world if I don't go all out for Christmas this year. I'm not exactly in the holiday spirit."

Barbara ran her finger down Scottie's cheek. "I know it's tough, sweetie. Just hang in there. You'll get your baby soon."

As if on cue, the faint sound of a baby crying came from down the hall. Barbara's eyes grew round, like chocolate peppermint patties. For the first time, she noticed the can of formula on the kitchen counter. "What's going on, Scottie? Is there something you haven't told me?"

"Like what, Mom? Like God dropped a baby down from heaven into my arms." Scottie kept a straight face despite the irony in her words. "Anna asked me to babysit for Emily while she's at the dentist."

"That's pretty inconsiderate of her," Barbara said.

"Pu-lease! You know Anna better than that. She was in a jam because her sitter got sick at the last minute."

All of her closest friends had babies, but Anna was the only one who considered Scottie's feelings. On Saturday afternoons and evenings, which were the loneliest times for Scottie, Anna's husband often took care of their daughter while Anna went shopping or to the movies and dinner with Scottie. And she was always careful to avoid baby-centered topics of conversation.

Scottie took her mother by the arm and ushered her to the front door. "I'll see you Christmas Eve." She leaned in and gave her mother a peck on the cheek. "Do you need me to bring something?"

Barbara dismissed Scottie's offer with a wave of her gloved hand. "The Yellow Umbrella is catering the dinner for me. Bring Brad, if you must. And make sure that rascal brother of yours is on time for a change."

Scottie opened the door for her mother.

"I'll see you before then," Barbara said over her shoulder as she took off down the sidewalk.

"I have no doubt about that," Scottie mumbled, and closed the door against the cold.

4

S cottie dashed up the stairs to the nursery where she found baby Mary lying in a pool of spit-up, her sleeper soaked through with poop.

"Oh, honey, is your little tummy upset?" Scottie unzipped the sleeper, peeled the fabric back, and carried the baby at arm's length to the changing table. She cleaned the baby from head to toe with baby wipes and dressed her in the second largest baby outfit, the only one she had left that would fit her. "I guess we better go on that shopping trip sooner rather than later."

She stripped the crib of the soiled linens, and carried them downstairs to the laundry closet. With the baby sucking hard on her thumb in the crook of her arm, Scottie opened her laptop on the kitchen counter and began to surf the Internet with her free hand.

"Now. Let's see what Mr. Google says about your upset tummy. My guess is, your mama's been breastfeeding you. Hopefully, it's just a transitional issue." The fingers of her right hand slid across the keyboard. "Yep"—she pointed at the screen as she read—"says here, the doctors recommend trying a new formula for at least three days before switching." She closed the laptop and looked down at the baby. "Don't go getting sick on me, little Mary. I don't know how I would explain your sudden appearance in my life to the pediatrician. Even if he is my best friend's husband."

Merry Mary smiled at her from behind her thumb.

Aside from her chapped cheeks, the baby appeared healthy, which was amazing considering she'd been living outdoors. Not to mention the recent snowstorm and subzero temperatures. Who knew what was written in the medical histories of the biological parents? Or what kind of addiction issues the mother had passed along to Mary? She didn't appear to have any abnormalities, but one could never be too sure in these situations.

Although the image of the dead woman's face would forever be imprinted on Scottie's mind, the woman's condition made it difficult to determine whether she'd been attractive. Scottie viewed Mary as a lovely baby with her bright blue eyes and pert little nose, as pretty as any mother would hope for her own little girl.

Mary seemed content to ride along in the baby carrier strapped to Scottie's torso, facing out, while she brought down the bouncy seat and other equipment from the nursery. As soon as the daycare center was organized in the family room, Mary began to fuss for her bottle.

Scottie fed and burped her, then fastened her in the bouncy seat in front of the Christmas tree. "There now," she said, running her hand across the blonde peach fuzz atop Mary's head. "You look at the pretty lights while I go to the attic for the ornaments to decorate this tree."

Racing up and down the stairs, Scottie made four trips to the attic for the Christmas decorations. She let the baby touch every shiny ornament before placing it on the tree. She was teetering on the stepladder, trying to attach the star to the top of the tree, when Mary had another blowout. Scottie quickly changed the diaper and started another load of laundry. In an attempt to stay calm, she reminded herself that the online doctor had advised against switching formulas before the baby's digestive system had a chance to adjust.

The afternoon dragged on, long lonely hours on a cold, gray day. No wonder her friends scheduled playdates every afternoon. While the baby napped in her Pack 'n Play, Scottie removed the photographs in her *Lost Souls* series from the walls and replaced them with contemporary paintings she'd created in her art classes at UVA—splashes of bright colors that resembled nothing but went a long way toward cheering up the room. She watched the Doctor Duo on television—Oz followed by Phil—folded a load of laundry, then thumbed through several of the baby care books she'd received as shower gifts. Desperate for adult conversation, she was happy to hear her husband's voice when he called around five.

"Uh, babe . . . I hate to tell you this, but I forgot to pay the power bill. I got an email notification. If we don't pay it by noon tomorrow, they're going to disconnect our service."

Scottie jumped to her feet. "Are you kidding me, Brad? That's the one bill you're responsible for paying. How could you let it go past due?" Early on in their marriage, when it became apparent Scottie would be the major breadwinner, they'd decided he would take care of the power, cable, and Internet bills, and she would pay for everything else. Considering how much he liked his electronics and gadgets, she felt confident he would keep these bills current.

Would he ever stop disappointing her?

He breathed loudly into the phone. "Okay, don't be mad. I really messed up, babe. Commonwealth Power has always given me an extension before. I don't understand why they're playing hardball this time. But they're threatening to turn the power off if they don't get full payment by noon tomorrow."

Scottie ran her hand through her tangled curls. "Are you telling me you don't have the money to pay the bill?"

He sighed. "I used it to buy my plane ticket."

"How much is the bill, Brad? I don't have an extra hundred dollars lying around."

"According to the email, we owe five hundred and eleven dollars," he said.

"Wait a minute, what? Our bill has never been that high."

"Actually, we're three months past due. I'm so sorry. I really screwed up this time."

"That's just great, Brad. I have exactly six hundred in my savings account." She imagined herself shivering under a mountain of blankets with the baby curled up next to her, hardly any different than living in a makeshift tent in Monroe Park. "Where's the bill? I'll pay it first thing in the morning."

"Well . . . would you believe me if I told you the dog ate it?"

She imagined his silly smile, the oops-I-messed-up-but-you-gotta-love-me-anyway grin she once found so charming. "We don't have a dog, Brad." She started to hang up but added, "Oh, and Brad, you can forget about getting a Christmas present from me."

She threw her phone down on the leather chair across from her. Her husband was not the same man she'd married, the guy with the 3.8 GPA in premed, who graduated in the top third of his class from UVA. That guy had had a bright future ahead of him as an orthopedist. After graduation, he'd taken a part-time job bartending to allow for more time to study for the MCAT. But that part-time soon became full-time with all thoughts of medical school forgotten.

Scottie's feelings about her husband and her career and starting a family stayed in constant conflict with one another. Her body was a battlefield of emotions, the North versus the South all over again. The sensible part of her, her brain, encouraged her to leave her husband and move to Washington or New York where the big photojournalists play ball. The emotional side of her, from her neck on down—including her heart where the souls of her future children resided and her empty womb where her biological clock ticked like a time bomb—ached for a baby. The gnawing sensation in her gut, the one she should trust but rarely did, cautioned her about bringing a baby into their crazy lives. Scottie traveled two, three, sometimes four days a week investigating breaking news stories. Daycare was out of the question with Brad working most nights. They'd have to hire a sitter, which would eat into his nominal take-home pay.

If he'd followed through on his original plan, he would be finishing up his residency right about now and looking for a practice to join. Instead, he was living paycheck to paycheck, using the money for their electric bill to pay for an airline ticket to visit his worthless family.

The first red flag for Scottie had been the ease in which Brad settled into the lifestyle of a bartender. The late hours suited him and he seemed to gain something from listening to other peoples' problems. Perhaps the satisfaction of knowing his life wasn't as screwed up as some. She'd encouraged him to consider psychiatry, but he seemed none too eager to return to the classroom. Academically, he'd burned himself out in high school and college, and he simply couldn't handle the daunting task of returning to the classroom.

She'd seen glimpses of the old Brad when she was pregnant. He'd made strides to find a better-paying job by updating his resume and interviewing for sales positions at several medical supply companies. He'd been devastated when Scottie lost the baby. She wasn't a quitter, and she didn't want to give up on her marriage. If only they could have a healthy baby . . .

Noticing Mary staring up at her from the Pack 'n Play, Scottie said, "But that's nothing for you to worry about, little one. I've dealt with worse crises than a past-due bill." She lifted the baby out of the playpen. "Are you getting hungry? I could use a cup of tea."

She poured Enfamil into a bottle for Mary and brewed a cup

of chai tea for herself, then settled with the baby on the couch to watch the local six o'clock news.

To her relief, there was no mention of a dead body in Monroe Park.

Mary sucked down two more small bottles and had three explosive bowel movements before Scottie finally put her down a few minutes before eleven. She turned on the television in her bedroom and listened to the late news while washing her face and brushing her teeth. At the very end of the newscast, the female anchor reported the discovery of an unidentified body in Monroe Park. The announcement lasted less than a minute with no mention of the victim's gender, the time of discovery, or a missing baby.

Relieved, Scottie slid beneath her thick duvet cover, rolling onto her side and curling up to her pillow. She tossed and turned with worry, and not just about the baby's gastrointestinal problems. She'd disclosed too much to her mother about her whereabouts that morning. Barbara was a curious, resourceful woman. If and when the missing baby made the news, she would know the crying she'd heard was not Emily.

Scottie finally gave up and crawled in the twin bed in the nursery. Comforted by the closeness of the baby, she fell fast asleep within minutes.

5

Scottie woke at dawn the following morning with the urgent need to pee. She rushed down the hall to the master bathroom and relieved herself. Removing her pocket calendar from her makeup drawer, she marked through the day's date with a red ballpoint pen. One more day. She always waited until she was five days late before taking a pregnancy test.

When she returned to the nursery, Mary was staring bright-eyed at the colorful zoo animals on the mobile above her. The baby had made it through the night without another blowout.

"I'll bet you're starving, Merry Mary," she said as she was changing her diaper. "I know I am. A bottle for you, cereal for me, then we'll go out and run our errands."

The approaching winter storm took precedence over all other news stories on the morning broadcast. Six to eight inches of snow was expected, starting around noon. Richmond often made it through the entire winter without any snow. For the city to get back-to-back storms in the month of December was rare.

"We need to hurry if we want to get home before the storm sets in." The baby stopped sucking and looked up at Scottie, as if she was waiting for her to continue. "We're going shopping, little girl, for all the latest winter fashions for babies." Scottie set the bottle on the table beside her and placed Mary over her shoulder to burp. "You need a snowsuit and a few more sleepers. And lots of diapers in the right size."

In an effort to avoid anyone who might recognize her and ask questions about the sudden appearance of a baby, Scottie drove to the Southside to pay her power bill at a designated payment center before traveling in the opposite direction to the Target at Virginia Center Commons. She placed Mary's car seat in the cart and piled the items she selected around her—sleepers and gowns in soft cotton; several packages of long-sleeved onesies, diapers, and formula; and a white snowsuit with fake gray trim around the hood. She even splurged on a festive set of baby mittens, a red-and-white retro pattern of snowflakes, which reminded her of a pair she'd owned as a child. She grabbed a carton of milk and a bag of Caesar salad from the grocery section, then stopped by the pharmacy to pick up a pregnancy test on her way out.

The first few flakes of snow were beginning to fall when she pulled up to the curb in front of her house. She was starting to take out the baby's car seat when a woman appeared at her side. An unkempt old woman in a threadbare coat and stocking cap. A woman she recognized as Mabel.

Scottie took a step back. Up close, the old woman smelled like cigarettes, rotten breath, and body odor.

Mabel wrapped her gnarled fingers around Scottie's wrist. "Nice-looking baby you got there. You aiming to keep her?"

Heart pounding against ribcage, Scottie jerked her hand away. "I don't know what you're talking about." She tried to block the baby from the woman's view.

"Look, Camera Lady, that baby's mama was a friend of mine. The others, they sent me to check you out, make sure you got what you need to take care of the baby." Forcing Scottie out of the way, Mabel leaned in the car to see the baby. She tickled

Mary's chin with her dirt-caked fingernail. "Trisha wouldn't want her daughter in no foster home."

Scottie's eyes searched the street for onlookers. "Listen. It's cold out here. Why don't you come inside where we can talk in private? I can offer you something warm to eat."

Mabel darted a quick glance at the town house, then looked away.

"I don't know about you, but I could use a cup of coffee." Leaving her purchases for later, Scottie pulled out the car seat and closed the door.

Mabel trudged after her up the sidewalk and through the house to the kitchen. Scottie strapped the baby in the bouncy seat and went to the refrigerator for a container of homemade Brunswick stew she'd purchased earlier in the week at Libbie Market.

"Please, have a seat"—Scottie gestured at the barstools —"while I warm up some soup."

Mabel lowered herself to the edge of the seat, clutching her ratty backpack to her chest. "I worked in a nice house like this once. The baby is lucky to have found you."

Scottie dumped the stew in a saucepan on the stove and turned on the burner. "I have no intention of keeping the baby. I didn't know what else to do when the rest of you left me alone with that poor woman's body. I made the split-second decision to bring the baby here, to get her out of the cold and into a warm house. I'll turn her over to the police as soon as they find her family."

The old woman glared at her. "Ain't no family to find."

"What do you mean? Everyone has a family."

"Trisha done a good job of getting herself lost after her daddy got liquored up and beat the living daylights outta her. Way I hear it, he nearly killed her."

Scottie swallowed hard. "That's horrible. What about her mother?"

"A drunk, just like her daddy."

"How long ago did, uh, Trisha run away from home?" Associating a name with the dead woman's face brought the reality of the situation down upon her.

Mabel shrugged. "Ten years, maybe. Her name ain't even Trisha as far as I know."

Scottie stirred the soup and set the Keurig to brew coffee. "What about the baby's father?"

Mabel dug through her backpack for a dirty tissue to wipe her nose. "Who knows who the baby's daddy is? Could be one of many."

"Was Trisha on drugs?"

"Nah. She what'n that kinda kid. She minded her own business. Never bothered nobody."

"Cream and sugar in your coffee?" Scottie asked when the Keurig had finished brewing.

"Black's fine. Ain't tasted cream-and-sugar coffee in years. Fancy fixings are for indoor living."

Scottie placed a cup of coffee and a bowl of stew in front of Mabel, and sat down beside her with a cup for herself, fully loaded with cream and sugar. "What happened that forced you to the streets, if you don't mind my asking?"

"My family was killed in a fire in the projects." Scottie's eyes grew wide, and Mabel added, "Every last one of 'em—husband, five kids, my sistah, a brother, and my mama. Hard to care about much after something like that happens to you."

"There are plenty of programs in Richmond that'll help you start a new life."

"What good's a new start gonna do an eighty-year-old woman like me?" Gripping her backpack close to her body with her left hand, Mabel scooped up a spoonful of soup with her right and gnawed on a piece of meat with the few teeth she had left.

Scottie reached across the island for her purse. "Here, let me give you something to help." She had only forty dollars left after paying the power bill, but this woman clearly needed it more.

Mabel held up her hand. "Nah, I didn't come here for money. I came here 'bout the baby."

Scottie looked over at Mary, who was quietly playing with the toy bar on the bouncy seat. "She's so quiet. Is she always so good?"

"Pretty much." Mabel set her spoon down in the soup bowl and wiped her mouth with her sleeve, ignoring the napkin Scottie had given her. "She won't be no trouble for you. What's one more mouth to feed when you already got a litter?" she asked as she glanced around the room.

Realizing that Mabel had made an assumption based on all the baby paraphernalia, Scottie said, "I don't have any children. At least not yet." She set the two twenties on the counter in front of Mabel. "I lost a baby back in the spring, which is why I have all this stuff."

Mabel reached for Scottie's hand, her calloused fingers rough against Scottie's soft palm. "God bless you, girl. I never have understood the ways of the Lord. So many needy chil'run running around the world when fine folks like you have empty homes."

Scottie blinked back the tears. "I haven't seen anything on the news. Do the police know about the baby?"

"If they do, they ain't heard it from us."

"They'll be able to tell from the autopsy, if they don't already know," Scottie said.

"Whatcha talking about, Camera Lady?" Mabel said, raising an unkempt eyebrow at Scottie. "The City ain't wasting their money on no autopsy for the homeless."

"That doesn't mean I can keep this baby, Ma—" Scottie stopped herself from calling the woman Mabel. "I'm sorry. I don't even know your name."

"It's better that way." The old woman slurped down another

spoonful of stew. "Give me one good reason you can't keep the baby. You got a nice home and a fine-looking husband." She aimed a gnarled finger at a group of photographs on the table beside the sofa.

"I can't keep a child that doesn't belong to me," Scottie said. "How would I prove she's mine?"

"You can buy anything you need on the street. Drugs. Documents. Somebody to off your husband if you need the life insurance."

"And when the police find out I took the baby, they'll charge me with kidnapping. Can I buy a Get Out of Jail Free card on this street corner you're talking about?"

"You ain't listening to me, girl." Mabel's nostrils flared. "The five-o don't know nothing 'bout the baby."

"Okay, listen." Scottie held her palms out as a signal for the old woman to settle down. "My husband's out of town. He doesn't even know about the baby yet. I'll get in touch with you once I make my decision."

Mabel got to her feet. "Decision's done been made for you. Yest'day, when the Lord sent you to the park to find this baby." The old woman turned her back on Scottie and headed down the hall to the front of the house.

"Wait a minute." Scottie caught up with her. "What's the baby's name?"

"Ain't got no name. Trisha just called her baby."

"You mean there's no name on the birth certificate?"

Mabel shook her head in despair. "I mean there's no birth certificate. We delivered the baby in the park ourselves, four months ago on August 24, hottest day of the year."

6

S cottie watched Mabel walk down the sidewalk in the snow until she was out of sight. She closed the door and leaned against it for support.

Was she seriously considering raising this child as her own?

Who are you kidding, Scottie? The idea has been in the back of your mind from the beginning, waiting for encouragement from you to emerge.

To avoid thinking about Mabel's visit, Scottie focused on unpacking the car, putting away her purchases, and straightening the kitchen. She was shocked to see the twenty-dollar bills still sitting on the counter. Disappointed, because she wanted to do something nice for the old woman, but humbled by the realization that nothing she could do would help.

She studied Mary's sweet face as she was feeding her a bottle. Why hadn't Trisha named her baby? Did she have some kind of premonition about her own death? Was she avoiding bonding with the child, knowing Child Protective Services might take her away? How sad, not only that this innocent child had no name but that she'd lived the first months of her life in filth. With no record of her birth, Mary did not exist, as least not as far as the Commonwealth of Virginia was concerned.

How was it fair that homeless women gave birth to nameless children when intelligent women of reasonable means suffered miscarriage after miscarriage?

By the time Scottie had finished feeding and bathing the baby, she was ready for a hot shower and a rest. Dressed in yoga pants and one of Brad's UVA sweatshirts, she started a load of laundry, made herself a chicken salad sandwich, and stretched out on the couch with the new John Grisham novel. When Mary woke around three o'clock, at least two inches of snow had fallen, with more on the way according to the radar. Scottie dressed Mary in one of her new outfits, a soft pink sleeper with an angel embroidered on the front. Despite the lack of natural daylight, she snapped dozens of photographs of the baby in different positions around the family room—images for Scottie to remember her by in the event she had to give her back.

When the doorbell rang around five, Scottie tiptoed to the front of the house and peeked through the peephole. She opened the door for her brother. "What're you doing here, Will?"

He stumbled into the foyer with a six-pack of Miller Lite tucked under his arm. Snow coated his dark hair, like vanilla icing on a chocolate cake. "I got stranded. Can I crash on your couch tonight?"

"Where's your car?"

"In the parking deck at work." He wriggled out of his Barbour coat and kicked his boots off in the corner. "The office closed because of the weather, so Hank and I decided to go to Sullivan's for an early happy hour."

She glanced at her watch. "You mean a late lunch. It's only five fifteen now." As much as she loved her younger brother, she occasionally found his party-time attitude tiresome. Will worked as an analyst for one of the brokerage firms by day, but at night he turned into a playboy. He needed to find a nice girl and settle down. "Did you walk all the way here from Sullivan's?"

He shook his head. "Hank gave me a ride."

"Why didn't he just take you home?"

"Because he was headed in the opposite direction." He yanked a lock of her hair. "What's the matter, aren't you happy to see me?" Without waiting for her answer, Will took off down the hallway toward the back of the house.

"Will, wait," she called after him. "You can't just come busting in here anytime you please."

He stopped dead in his tracks when he saw the baby bobbing up and down in her bouncy seat. "What's that?" Will asked, pointing at Mary as though he'd never seen a baby.

"A baby. Duh."

"Yeah, but whose?"

"Anna's, you idiot. That's Emily," Scottie said, surprised at how easy the lies flowed from her lips. "I'm babysitting for her while Anna's out of town."

Will narrowed his eyes. "I thought Emily had dark hair."

"No. She has blonde hair like her grandmother."

He looked doubtful. "I know for a fact that Anna's mother's hair is gray."

"Maybe now it is, but her hair was blonde before she got old." Scottie took the six-pack of beer from him and set it on the kitchen counter.

"Speaking of Anna's mother, why isn't Lula keeping Emily?"

"I don't know, Will. What's with the million questions? Lula is probably in New York having her gray hair styled or finishing her Christmas shopping."

He knelt down in front of Mary. "You sure are a cute little thing. Yes you are," he said in the same goo-goo voice he used with his hunting dogs. Mary offered him a toothless grin and he chucked her chin. "I think she likes me."

Scottie rolled her eyes. "Most women do."

Will straightened. "I'm starving. Will you make me a pizza?"

"I never said you could stay, Will. I'm kind of in the middle of something, in case you haven't noticed." She reached across the counter for her cell phone. "Why don't I order you an Uber?"

He laughed. "Don't bother. Thanks to the weather, there's at least a two-hour wait for Uber." He popped open a Miller Lite and took a long swill. "I'll find a ride home from somebody, after you feed me."

"Fine." She yanked open the freezer door. "But the dough will take a few minutes to thaw." She removed the plastic-wrapped ball of dough and submerged it in a sink full of warm water.

"That gives me time to get acquainted with Emily." Will turned on Scottie's whole-house audio system, unstrapped the baby from the bouncy seat, and danced her around the room to the music of Glen Miller's *In the Christmas Mood*. Mary threw back her head and belly laughed with glee.

"Careful you don't drop her, Will. You don't have a lot of experience with babies." Her tone was warning, but she couldn't help but smile. Her brother acted like a child himself at times.

Will continue to twirl Mary about the room while Scottie rolled out the dough and covered it with tomato sauce, layers of mozzarella cheese, and pepperoni. After sliding the pizza into the preheated oven, she held her arms out for Mary. "Give me the baby, Will. You're making her dizzy."

To Will's delight, the baby burst into tears when he handed her to Scottie.

"He's no good for you, Mary. He'll break your heart and leave you in a puddle of tears."

Will dropped his smile as his body grew still. "Did you just call the baby Mary?"

"I don't know, did I?" Scottie turned her back on him so he couldn't see the fear in her eyes. She busied herself with making a bottle. "I hold a lot of babies when I volunteer in the nursery at church."

When her remark seemed to pacify him, he slid onto a barstool and popped open another beer. "I'm not sure all this babysitting is such a good idea, Scottie. I don't want to see you get hurt. You've already been through so much."

She waved away his concern with a flick of the wrist. "You don't need to worry about me. I can handle it." She took the baby and the bottle to the sofa across the room. Patting the cushion beside her, she said, "Come, talk to me while I feed Emily."

He joined her on the sofa. "What's different about this room?" He looked around at the bright paintings on the wall. "It's warm and cozy in here, happy even." He snapped his fingers. "I know what it is. You finally took down those depressing photographs."

"Art is intended to move the observer. If the photographs of my homeless people depress you, I've done my job. At least I know the title of my series, *Lost Souls*, is well suited."

"It's not that your photographs aren't good. I just think looking at them day in and out might bring you down. Why don't you hang them in a gallery somewhere?"

"I'm working on it."

"When is Anna coming back, anyway? You're not taking care of Emily all weekend, are you?"

"Maybe. David's mother is in the hospital. They drove up to Baltimore to see her. They only planned to be gone overnight, but with this weather, they may need to stay longer." Guilt washed over Scottie as she buried herself in yet another layer of lies.

"What's wrong with David's mother?"

"I'm not sure, something about an irregular heartbeat."

Will spread his arms wide at all the baby stuff cluttering the room. "Not that I really care, but how does Brad feel having his home turned into *Romper Room*?"

"He doesn't know."

Will squeezed his eyes shut, then opened them again. "What do you mean, he doesn't know?"

"He's in California visiting his family. See, having Emily here is a good thing. She's keeping me company while he's gone."

"I'm surprised you aren't covering the mall shooting in Kentucky," he said.

What mall shooting in Kentucky? She'd been so preoccupied with the baby she hadn't watched the national news or looked at social media in twenty-four hours. Staying on top of breaking news was vital to her success.

Scottie managed to keep a straight face. "I'm taking some time off for the holidays."

Will studied her closely, as if searching for the truth. They weren't in the habit of lying to one another. Scottie seldom took time off from her job, her one element of gratification in an otherwise dismal existence.

Will burped the baby while Scottie got up to remove the pizza from the oven. He ate four slices and exchanged texts with his fan club while she finished feeding Mary her bottle.

"I'm worried about you, sis," he said, tossing his last bite of crust on his plate and setting it on the coffee table. "I'm not buying this baby thing. I know you well, and you are not a good liar." Their eyes locked, and they communicated in their silent understanding the way they'd done all their lives. She wasn't ready to tell him the truth, even though she knew he'd support her regardless of her crime.

"I appreciate your concern, Will, but everything is fine. The only problem we have to worry about is what to give Mom for Christmas.

He grimaced. Shopping for their mother was the most stressful part of the holidays. She already owned everything she needed or wanted. Yet the one year she'd insisted they save their money—and they'd complied—she made them suffer until Easter.

The doorbell rang and Scottie jumped up, ready to escape the backdoor with the baby.

"Chillax, Scott, that's just my ride." He kissed her cheek before he rose to leave. "If you need me, call me. You have my number."

"Me, and every other woman on the planet."

Scottie buried her head in the sand by avoiding all sources of the news, both local and worldwide, the television as well as the pinging and dinging of her cell phone. She didn't want to hear about the dead body found in Monroe Park any more than she wanted to be alerted when the police discovered the baby missing. Mabel had planted the seed of hope that she might be able to keep the baby, and her overactive imagination was providing the fertilizer for that seed to grow. With any luck, the whole situation would blow over. The medical examiner would save taxpayer dollars and declare the cause of death hypothermia without performing an autopsy. The police would drop their investigation, and Scottie would pay a thousand dollars for a forged birth certificate that claimed Mary Evelyn Darden the daughter of Virginia Scott Westport Darden and Bradford James Darden.

7

"Scottie rushed to the toilet and shoved the pregnancy test stick between her legs to catch the stream of her concentrated morning pee. She set the stick on the counter and paced in tiny circles while she waited for the results. When a blue plus sign appeared, she dropped to the floor and hugged her knees to her chest. Her excitement was clouded by dread of the long months ahead. The constant fear of miscarriage and the anxious visits to the doctor. How would she survive another heartbreak?

When she heard the baby cry, she went to her, lifting her from her crib and holding her tight. "Hear that, little one. You're going to have a baby sister or a brother." A thought occurred to her. "If it's a boy, the two of you will be Irish twins like Will and me. Isn't that exciting?"

The baby grinned a toothless grin, then poked out her lower lip and began to cry for her bottle.

The storm had moved out of the area overnight, but the sky was still gray. The roads would remain slick with temperatures not expected to rise above thirty. "Looks like we're stuck inside today, Merry Mary. Might as well make the most of it."

Mary bounced up and down in her bouncy seat and stared at the lights on the Christmas tree while Scottie worked in Photoshop scrolling through her images of the *Lost Souls*. She needed only two more photographs to complete her homeless series before she could contact an old college friend who managed a gallery in New York. As depressing as the images were, she was proud of her work for arousing such poignant emotion. If she could sell several of the photographs, or perhaps the entire series to a collector, she could earn enough money to stay home with the baby while she figured out her next career move. With a major in communication and a minor in political science and current affairs, she had choices other than photojournalism. Any number of jobs would allow her to work from home, even if she temporarily took a job blogging for one of the major news networks.

As the day dragged on, the idea appealed to her more and more. Pen and paper in hand, she devised her plan to convince Brad they should keep the baby. Weather permitting, his flight would arrive late in the afternoon on Sunday. She would greet him at the door with a glass of his favorite wine and usher him into the now-cozy family room. He would be putty in her hands with the fire burning, the Christmas tree glowing, and the baby cooing softly in her playpen. After she explained Mary's presence in their house, she would feed him his favorite dinner—homemade lasagna, Caesar salad, and garlic bread—while she presented her case. Scottie aimed to have her way. She would pull out the big guns if necessary. As much as he disliked the idea of adoption, he would be even more opposed to her going to jail for kidnapping, particularly when he learned about the pregnancy.

After Mary's two o'clock feeding, Scottie strapped her in the baby swing in front of the television. She found a station airing reruns of classic Christmas cartoons—*Rudolph*, the original version of *How the Grinch Stole Christmas*, and Scottie's personal favorite, *The Year without a Santa Claus* starring the Heat Miser.

Scottie baked a batch of sugar cookies and Brad's favorite dessert —a red velvet cake.

Will showed up out of the blue a few minutes after six with a bottle of red wine and a tray of sushi. His expression grew serious when he saw Mary playing with a rattle in the playpen. "Why is she still here?"

"I told you, there was a chance I'd have her for the whole weekend. With the snowstorm and all, Anna and Dave decided to stay another night."

Will opened the wine, poured two glasses, and handed one to her. "I really don't think this is such a good idea, Scott. You're still vulnerable after losing the baby."

"I'm fine, Will." She set her wine glass down on the counter without taking a sip. "I appreciate your concern, but you don't need to worry about me."

He stared at her hard, an uncomfortable glare that made her squirm. He didn't believe she was fine anymore than he believed the baby belonged to Anna and Dave.

Scottie lifted the lid on the sushi tray. The pungent smell of seafood brought about a wave of nausea that she recognized as her first official symptom of pregnancy.

"Here, have some." She slid the tray across the counter to Will. "I'm not hungry."

"Save it for later, then. I have a dinner date at nine."

Her eyes grew wide. "Do tell."

Will sat down next to Scottie. Knowing his sister wouldn't let him off the hook until he gave her the facts, he spit out his date's bio in one long breath. "Name's Elise Bingham; originally from Greenwich, Connecticut; graduated summa cum laude from MIT; works as a systems analyst for DACOR Corporation. She's working part-time at the Apple Store during the holidays, hence the reason we're having dinner so late."

"Let me get this straight. You, the guy who is only attracted to lawyers and stockbrokers, have a date with a computer nerd?"

He shrugged. "She's the hottest computer nerd I've ever seen. I'm telling you, Scott, this girl is pretty and smart. She might be the one."

"So tell me," Scottie said, propping her elbows on the counter. "How did you meet this Elise?"

"We met last night at the Tobacco Company," he said, and took a big gulp of wine.

Scottie's jaw dropped open. "You met her in a loud and crowded bar and you think she's the one? How could you even hear what she was saying?" She paused, thinking. "Wait a minute. We were having a snowstorm last night. I'm surprised the Tobacco Company was even open. And you were already half-baked when you left here around seven."

"I took a nap before going back out. And the Tobacco Company wasn't crowded because of the weather, which offered the opportunity for meaningful conversation."

Scottie glanced at the clock on the wall oven. "You can't stay here until nine. I have to bathe Mar . . ."—she caught herself —"the baby and put her to bed."

Their eyes met and they began to stare each other down. Scottie was the first to look away. She'd invented the staring game when they were little. And she almost always won.

He sighed. "I hope I'm the one you call when you decide to come clean about this baby."

Her chin quivered and tears sprang to her eyes.

Will stood and pulled her to her feet. Wrapping his arms around her, he rubbed her back for a while. "Okay, then." He held her at arm's length. "Change of subject. What say we give Mom an iPad for Christmas?"

Scottie smiled through her tears and play-punched his arm. "You're just looking for an excuse to go out to the Apple Store early."

"No, seriously. Think about it. An iPad would open up a whole new avenue of shopping for Mom." While their mother was no technology expert, she considered herself a professional shopper.

"I don't know, Will. An iPad doesn't exactly fit in my budget this year."

"No worries." He brushed off her concern as he headed down the hall to the front door. "You can pay me back with the money Mom and Dad give you for Christmas."

She opened the door for him. "At least we don't have to worry about Dad." At Will's insistence, they had purchased a dozen top-of-the-line goose decoys for their father when they were on sale during the summer. "And since I'm giving my husband electricity for Christmas, I only have one more present to buy. Yours."

He smirked. "I'm not sure I want to know what kind of electricity you're giving Brad."

"Trust me, you don't."

"You know what I want, right?" He winked at her.

"Of course." She leaned up and kissed his cheek. "I saved the link you sent me with the size, brand, color, and style number."

He tugged on a lock of her hair. "I'm only teasing you, sis. If money is tight, please don't buy me anything."

"I'm not destitute, Will. At least not yet."

8

S unday dawned with bright skies and warmer temperatures. Scottie hated to miss the Christmas service at St. James, but she couldn't very well show up at church with an unexplained baby. She would spend her day finishing her shopping and preparing for Brad's homecoming.

During Mary's morning nap, she lounged on the sofa in her pajamas with a steaming mug of cocoa watching Christmas movies on the Lifetime channel. When the baby woke around eleven, she fed her a bottle, bundled her in warm clothes, and took off up the interstate to the north side of town. Knowing she would undoubtedly run into one of her father's or brother's friends, she bypassed Green Top—a specialty hunting and fishing store where all the locals shopped—and continued on I 95 to the Bass Pro Shop in Ashland. After circling several times, she finally found a parking spot at the far edge of the crowded lot.

I should have brought the stroller, she thought, as she hauled the heavy car seat across the wet asphalt to the store. She encountered a mob scene inside with people standing in long lines at check-out counters, scrutinizing apparel, and seeking advice from the sales staff on hunting and fishing merchandise. There was even a crowd of children waiting impatiently to visit with a camouflage-clad Santa Claus.

"Looks like we're on our own here, Merry Mary." Giving up on finding someone to help them, she hauled the car seat up the stairs to the second floor and through the maze of racks until she found the one displaying the Drake camouflage pullover Will had asked for.

"Lesson number one about consumer spending," she whispered to Mary as they waited in line at checkout. "Charge it to your credit card and worry about it in January."

On the way home, she stopped at Martin's in Glen Allen for the few items she needed for dinner, and at a street vendor in Carytown where she spent her last twenty dollars on a wreath for her door—a mixture of evergreens, plump holly berries, and a big fat red bow.

After she unloaded the car and got the baby settled, she spent the afternoon setting the ambiance for a romantic dinner. Brad's flight was on time. At exactly five-thirty, dressed in a red knit dress and strappy black heels, Scottie greeted him at the door with a glass of his favorite Malbec wine.

"Missed me, did you?" He pecked her cheek, then dumped his duffle at the bottom of the staircase. "I didn't realize you and I had plans for tonight. I promised some of the guys I'd meet them downtown in an hour."

They'd grown apart during the past two years. Coming and going on different schedules, they were more like roommates than husband and wife.

"I made dinner for you, Brad. I thought we could talk."

He ignored the glass of wine in her outstretched hand and headed toward the kitchen. She followed on his heels.

He passed the dining room with barely a glance at the candlelit table, but he noticed right away the transformation in the family room—flames flickering in the fireplace, the Christmas tree ablaze with lights, and the colorful paintings dotting the walls. "This is nice, babe. Feels like home. I can finally relax without those depressing vagabonds watching my every move."

Spotting the baby in her bouncy seat, he walked over and knelt down in front of her. "Whose kid? Are you babysitting for one of your friends?" He ruffled Mary's hair and she pouted her lower lip.

Scottie set the glass of wine on the counter and lifted the baby out of her bouncy seat. "No, Brad. That's what I need to talk to you about. The baby is ours."

His body grew still and his jaw went slack as he stared at her in disbelief for a long, awkward moment of silence. "I don't understand, Scottie. I thought I made it clear, I don't want to adopt a baby."

"But this is different. If you'll just give me a chance to explain."

Brad tossed his leather coat onto a nearby chair and went to the refrigerator for a beer. "I don't know how it could be different. Another man's child is another man's child." He spoke in a harsh tone.

Mary began to cry. "It's okay, sweetie. No need to cry," Scottie said, bouncing the baby up and down on her hip.

Brad unscrewed the cap with his teeth and downed half the bottle in one swig.

"Please, Brad. If you'll give me a chance to tell you what happened, you'll see that this baby is a gift from God. Call it a miracle, or divine intervention. Whatever you call it, she's our dream come true."

Brad glanced at the baby, then glared at Scottie. "Have you lost your mind?"

"There's nothing wrong with my mind." She raised her voice

and the baby began to wail in response. She popped the top off a formula bottle and shoved the nipple into Mary's mouth. "You'll understand what I'm talking about once you hear my story. Please, can we just sit down so I can explain?"

He glanced at his watch. "You have ten minutes, but I'm warning you that nothing you say will change the way I feel about adoption."

He plopped down in his leather chair next to the Christmas tree and she lowered herself to the sofa opposite him. Hoping to earn his confidence in her plan, she delivered in a calm voice the speech she'd rehearsed. She recounted her discovery of the dead body in the park and her split-second decision to bring the child to safety, away from the filth and outdoor elements of the home-less life, to protect her from a future of foster care. And she told him about Mabel's visit.

His face flushed red with anger. "You let a homeless person into our home."

"You're missing my point, Brad. That poor dead woman's friends know her baby will have a better life with us."

Brad listened, his resolute expression unwavering, as Scottie described in detail all the benefits they had to offer the baby.

"Need I remind you, Scottie, that we're broke."

"That's *your* fault, Brad, and it's only a minor setback. If we tighten our belt, stick to our budget for a change, we'll be fine. And my parents will help."

He pursed his lips and raised his voice, mocking her as he repeated, "My parents will help." He drained the rest of his beer and slammed the empty bottle on the coffee table.

Mary watched him out of the corner of her eye, but continued to suck on her bottle.

"You never seemed bothered by my parents' help before."

"A man has his pride, Scottie." He got up and went to the refrigerator for another beer.

"Brad this baby needs us. With no birth certificate, as far as the world is concerned, she doesn't exist. Some divine power from above dropped her in our laps. She's our Christmas miracle."

He opened his lips and poured the amber liquid down his throat. "I gotta say, Scottie, that's the most fucked-up, hocus-pocus nonsense I've ever heard."

"Exactly, which means it has to be true. Mary is a gift from God."

"Wait a minute. How do you know her name?"

"Her mother never gave her a name. I needed to call her something, so I came up with Merry Mary." Her eyes traveled from the nativity scene on the mantle to the Merry Christmas needlepoint pillow in the chair opposite her. "I admit it sounds kind of silly when I say it out loud. We can change it to whatever we want."

He set his bottle down and went to sit beside his wife. "Listen, babe. It's totally understandable considering all you've been through this year, but you've lost touch with reality. We need to get you some help. You're having some kind of delayed hormonal breakdown or something."

Scottie pulled the bottle away from the baby and jumped to her feet. "You haven't listened to a word I've said." She lifted the baby to the burp cloth on her shoulder and began smacking her back. "Why do men blame everything on hormones?"

"Calm down, honey. You're going to hurt the baby."

Scottie lightened her touch.

"Okay, listen." He tugged on her arm. "Sit back down, so we can talk about this."

Scottie dropped back down onto the sofa beside him.

He shifted his position to face her. "Do you realize you could go to prison for kidnapping?"

Scottie ignored his gaze, unable to bear the pity in his eyes. "I already told you, Brad. The police don't know about the baby."

"How can you be so sure these homeless people won't talk?"

"Because they believe this is what the mother would've wanted. They know we can give her a better home than anything she'd get in foster care."

"Why do you assume she'll go into foster care? She's an infant. Wouldn't she be placed in an orphanage where some nice young couple will adopt her?"

"I'm not willing to take that chance."

"You're impossible when you get like this." He stood up and began pacing back and forth in front of her, his hand chopping the air while he talked. "Okay, let's assume I'm willing to go along with you on this, which I'm not, but hypothetically speaking. How do you expect her to go through life without a birth certificate?"

Mary let out a giant burp, and Scottie stuck the bottle back in her mouth. "We'll buy one."

"And how do you suggest we do that?"

"I'm an investigative journalist, remember? I can find someone to sell us the documents."

He stopped for a minute, looked over at her, then started pacing again. "Great, so our daughter goes through life with a fake birth certificate. Next question—how are you planning to explain her sudden appearance to our friends and families?"

"I've thought it all through. We'll leave town, maybe drive up to New York. When we come back after the holidays, we'll tell everyone we arranged for a private adoption."

He nodded. "And how do you plan to finance this trip?"

Several snide remarks regarding their past-due power bill came to mind, but she held her tongue. No point in fueling his anger. "If we wait until after Christmas to leave, we can use the money my parents give me."

"And how will we explain our absence at your parents' Christmas Eve dinner?"

Scottie knew he was playing along with her, hoping she'd

eventually fall into her own trap. "You can stay home with the baby. We'll say you're sick." She was grasping at straws. Even her voice sounded desperate.

"At least one part of your plan makes sense. Your parents will be thrilled not to have to look at me across their dinner table."

"Brad . . . That's not true," she said, her voice soft.

"It is true, and we both know it." He stood in front of her, looking down on her. "You have a solution to all the problems except the biggest one."

"What's that?"

"The part about me not wanting to adopt a baby. You've dug your own grave this time, Scottie. I'll be damned if you're going to bury me with you."

Scottie's face tightened. "Don't make me choose. You might not like the outcome."

He stared at her, his mouth agape. "So you're going to choose a baby you know nothing about over me. Have you even given any thought to her health? For all we know, her mother was a meth addict. No telling what kind of brain damage or long-term health care she might need."

Scottie tuned her husband out. She'd already considered all the what-ifs. "That's a chance I'm willing to take."

"You're playing a dangerous game, babe. Get out while you still can."

She stood to face him. "And what do you suggest I do with her?"

"How the hell am I supposed to know? Take her back where you found her. Or leave her in the emergency room at one of the hospitals."

"And risk being caught by a video camera?"

"You should have thought about that before you kidnapped her."

When he reached for his coat and started toward the door,

Scottie knew it was time for her to drop the bomb. "You've made it clear how you feel about raising another man's child. How do you feel about having your own baby born in prison?"

9

Brad crawled into bed at daybreak on Monday. He curled up next to Scottie and wrapped his arm around her. Lifting her hair away from her ear, he whispered, "Are you awake?"

"I am now."

"I've been driving around all night thinking about the baby. Although I'm not totally sold on your plan, I believe we can offer her a good life." He let out a deep breath that tickled her neck. "I agree with you. The way she found her way into our lives seems like more than a coincidence. Maybe someone from above *did* place her in our lives for a reason."

Brad's parents were not churchgoing people. She'd often heard him say, "I can count on one hand the number of times I've been inside a church. Don't get me wrong. I believe in God. I just choose to worship him in my own way." Aside from their wedding ceremony, the one time she'd convinced him to go to church with her—several Easters ago—he'd claimed the high Episcopal service was smoke and mirrors.

Brad rolled Scottie onto her back. "Are you really pregnant again?" he asked, rubbing her flat stomach.

"Yep. And I'm scared to death."

He brushed a stray curl off her forehead. "Everything will be fine this time. I feel it in my bones."

"You said that last time, and look what happened."

When Brad tried to kiss her, Scottie turned her head away. "Don't, Brad. I'm not in the mood." She couldn't remember the last time they'd made sensual love together, like in the beginning of their relationship when they came together as one, like they were the only two people on the planet and the only thing that mattered was satisfying their hunger. The nights of drunken lust still happened—tearing each others clothes off and having ravenous sex on the floor in front of the fire or in the backseat before they even got out of the car—but she found it hard to get excited about Brad cramming his cigarette-and-beer tasting tongue down her throat first thing in the morning.

"Come on, baby, I missed you so much." He jammed his knee between her legs and began to paw at her pajamas.

"I said stop, Brad." She tried to shove him off of her, but she couldn't budge his two-hundred-pound body.

Scottie bit her lip until she tasted blood. She knew from experience it was best to grin and bear it. It would be over soon. Sex never lasted long anymore.

An hour later, Scottie was feeding Mary a bottle when, out of habit, she clicked on the television, forgetting about her self-imposed ban on the news. Standing at the entrance of the park, Joyce Jackson, a young African-American reporter announced, "The body of the young woman discovered in Monroe Park on Thursday of last week has been identified as twenty-one-year-old Melissa Sabin from Portland, Oregon."

So her name wasn't Trisha after all?

Joyce held her hand to her earpiece and listened while Mike Conrad, the newscaster in the studio, asked, "Any word on the cause of death?"

The reporter shook her head. "Not yet, Mike. The medical

examiner's office has promised preliminary autopsy results by the end of the day. We'll continue to follow this breaking story and have more for you at noon."

Panic gripped Scottie's chest. She leaned down and kissed Mary's forehead. "Don't worry. I won't let them take you from me."

She turned off the television. The autopsy would reveal that Melissa Sabin had recently given birth and was nursing a baby when she died. It wouldn't take the police long to realize the baby had gone missing from the scene. Human interest would escalate and every investigative reporter in the area would jump on the story. At twenty-one, Melissa Sabin was just a child herself. Scottie assumed her parents were the ones who identified the body. Would they try to gain custody of the baby? According to Mabel, they were both alcoholics and the father abusive. Mary was better off in foster care.

Scottie set the bottle on the coffee table and paced the room while she burped the baby. The scene unfolded in her head. The police would show up at her door. They'd handcuff Scottie and haul her off to jail while the neighbors watched from behind closed curtains. Mary would go to live with her alcoholic, abusive grandparents in Oregon while Scottie spent the next ten Christmases in a correctional center for women.

She placed her hand on her belly. She didn't stand a chance of carrying this baby to term under such stressful circumstances.

No way Brad would go along with adopting the baby now. He would turn Scottie into the police before he implicated himself in the kidnapping of a child he didn't even want. After his long flight from California and being up all night, he would probably sleep past noon. And since he wasn't a news junkie, as long as she kept the television turned off, he might not hear about the identification of the body until he went to work late that afternoon. Scottie figured she had until six o'clock, when the local news aired, to make her move. Until then, she needed to stay calm. To do that, she needed to keep busy.

She strapped Mary in the baby swing, opened her laptop, and created a new Word document. Her fingers flew across the keyboard as the words came to her. The story had been on her mind for months, and she needed to get her thoughts on paper while her feelings were still fresh.

She was seven hundred words in when Brad appeared in the kitchen. "Please don't tell me you're planning to post a story about the homeless on the Internet," he said, reading the document over her shoulder. "Connecting yourself to those homeless people is lunacy. You can never let anyone know about your relationship with those people in Monroe Park. Which means you can't sell your photographs either. All the time you spent on your series was wasted."

She slammed the laptop closed. He was right, of course. Her photographs would forever link her to Melissa Sabin. She'd been planning on using the proceeds from her series to start a new life. "I'm not stupid, Brad," she said, although she felt like an idiot. "I'm not planning to post my story. I just needed to get these thoughts off my chest." She went to the refrigerator and poured him a glass of orange juice. "Why are you up so early, anyway?"

He gulped down the juice, then licked his lips. "I'm working a double shift to make up for my vacation time. So don't wait up for me." He started down the hall toward the front of the house, then stopped. "I'm warning you, Scottie," he said, without turning around. "Don't get too attached to that baby. I haven't made up my mind about keeping her yet."

Don't get too attached? That was like telling an addict not to get hooked on heroin. Maybe not the best analogy, but it adequately described the way Scottie felt. She'd more than grown attached to the baby. Mary gave new purpose to her life. She filled a void inside of Scottie that had been empty for far too long.

Scottie only hoped Brad didn't force her to choose.

She glanced at the clock on the oven. Ten minutes before eleven. Almost time for the party to start. Anna's parents were throwing a party for Anna's friends and their children, complete with a magician dressed like Santa Claus. Go figure. Scottie had regretted her invitation, as if they'd actually expected her to come.

If only I can get through the day.

While the baby dozed in the swing, Scottie piddled around the house in her pajamas, trying not to think about what lay ahead for her. She did several loads of laundry and wrapped presents for her family, even though she wouldn't be around to hand them out on Christmas Eve. When Mary woke from her nap, Scottie gave her a bath, then left her in her crib to stare at the mobile while she showered. She dressed as if she had somewhere to go in a pair of designer jeans, her favorite cashmere sweater, and her tall black boots that Brad thought sexy.

The long hours of the afternoon loomed before her. Once she finalized Mary's adoption and the new baby was born, she would add more structure to her days. In the mornings, she would take the children on playdates or to run errands or to swim at the club during the summertime. She would work at her computer while they napped in the afternoons, then the three of them would go on long walks or special outings before dinner. She would mold her career to fit her new lifestyle, at least while the children were still little.

Scottie put the baby down for a nap after her two o'clock feeding. She then removed her rolling suitcase and a large duffle from the attic and filled them with clothes—several outfits plus underwear and toiletries in the rolling suitcase for herself, and everything she'd bought for the baby plus diapers, blankets, and burp cloths in the duffle for Mary. She stored both bags in the coat closet beside the front door, easy access for a quick escape.

With nothing to do but wait for the first edition of the local news at five, she browned a pound of ground beef and spooned it into a crockpot with the rest of the ingredients for a chili dinner no one would be home to eat. She wrote long letters on monogrammed stationery to her family. One for her mother and one for her father, which she would leave on the kitchen counter, and one to Will, which she would deliver in person. If her plan went accordingly, her parents would never read the letters, but if something went wrong, she wanted them to hear the story in her own words.

ary woke from her afternoon nap with a fever. "You're burning up, little girl. Can you tell me what hurts?" As Scottie lifted her from the crib, the baby threw up all over her cashmere sweater. Not your typical baby spit-up after a bottle feeding but the rancid vomit of the truly ill.

Mary began to cry, a pitiful moaning sound Scottie had not heard from her before.

The hairs stood up on Scottie's neck. She had yet to get to the chapter on childhood illnesses in her baby research. She didn't have any children's Tylenol or Motrin, not that she would know how to administer it. She snapped her fingers, remembering the fancy baby thermometer one of her mother's friends had given her at the shower. She found it in her supplies, ripped open the package, and inserted the thermometer in Mary's ear. When the thermometer beeped, its digital display read 102 degrees.

"Think, Scottie," she said out loud to herself.

She went to the bathroom and dampened a washcloth with cold water. She laid Mary on the changing table and rubbed her body all over with the wet cloth. She rinsed the washcloth and repeated the process several times. She picked the baby up and sank to the nearby rocker in despair. She wouldn't be able to leave town tonight. Taking a sick baby on the road was simply too dangerous.

Nothing seemed to relieve Mary's discomfort. She vomited three more times during the next hour and her fever spiked to one hundred and three degrees. Scottie tried rocking her and walking her around the house. She didn't think feeding her formula was a good idea, so she tried water in the bottle instead, which pacified Mary long enough for Scottie to watch the five o'clock news.

Wally Warner—the old man newscaster with a fake tan and gray hair glued to his head with hairspray—led off with the story Scottie had been dreading. "In the case of the twenty-one-year-old homeless woman discovered in Monroe Park on Thursday, the medical examiner has released the shocking autopsy report just minutes ago. Joyce Jackson has been following this story all day, and is standing by in Monroe Park." Joyce appeared the screen. "What can you tell us, Joyce?"

"Well, Wally, according to the medical examiner, the autopsy showed that the young woman, one Melissa Sabin, had recently given birth and was still nursing the baby at the time of her death." The camera panned to the scene behind her where police were questioning a group of bystanders. Scottie recognized Buck and Miss Cecil. "Sources tell police that Melissa Sabin was seen with the baby the evening before she died from hypothermia."

Great. Scottie turned off the television. Just when she thought things couldn't get worse. If even one of those homeless people broke their pledge, her Christmas goose was cooked. Scottie's phone vibrated on the coffee table with texts from Brad insisting she turn on the television, and from Will: *Please tell me the baby on the news isn't the one in your living room.*

She reached for the phone and thumbed a quick response: *IDK what u r talking about.*

Scottie considered her options. She could do as Brad suggested and leave Mary in the emergency room at one of the area hospitals—St. Mary's, perhaps, or VCU. At least the baby would get the medical attention she obviously needed. But then they'd capture her on the security camera and the footage would be played over and over on the national news, just like when the poor UVA student went missing last year. No judge would let her off the hook for anything less than ten years.

She could hand the baby over to the police and explain that she'd hadn't meant any harm, that she'd only been trying to offer the baby food and shelter until the body was identified. She looked down at Mary who was peering up at her through glassy eyes. "I don't like that option either, little one. No way am I giving you up that easily."

The third option, and the only one that made any sense to Scottie, was to take the baby and leave town until the whole thing died down. She would return with her birth certificate, and no one would ever know. And the case of the missing baby in Monroe Park would remain unsolved.

But first she needed to get Mary's fever down.

Scottie scrolled through her contacts and clicked on Anna's mobile number. She answered on the second ring. "We missed you at the party today, Scott. But I'm sure you had more pressing matters to attend to than watching babies fight over rattles."

"I'm sorry I couldn't make it. I'm babysitting for my cousin's little girl, which is why I'm calling. Is Dave home from work yet?"

"Not yet, but I expect him any minute. Why, what's wrong?"

"My cousin and her husband went to DC for the night. The baby is sick, vomiting with fever, and my cousin isn't answering her cell phone."

"How high is the fever?" Anna sounded concerned.

"A hundred and three."

"That doesn't sound good. You should probably take her to Patient First."

"I would, except my cousin forgot to leave me her insurance card. Or any medicine. I don't even have infant Tylenol."

"Okay, let me think a minute." Anna paused. "Dave should be home any minute. I'm sure he wouldn't mind running down to take a look at her."

"I'd bring her to you—"

"No, don't do that! It's cold out. You stay put, and we'll be there as soon as we can. Besides, this will give me a chance to bring you your Christmas present."

Scottie ended the call. Cradling Mary in the crook of her left arm, she dropped to her knees and crawled over to the Christmas tree. She searched through the presents until she found Anna's— a framed black-and-white photograph of Emily she'd taken at their Fourth of July picnic.

Mary started crying again and didn't let up until Anna and Dave arrived an hour later. Scottie was frantic when she handed the baby over to Dave.

"So this is your cousin's baby?" Laying her down on the sofa, he listened to her heart and lungs with his stethoscope.

Scottie nodded. "My cousin Elizabeth. She lives in North Carolina."

"That's funny. I've never heard you mention her." Anna sat down on the sofa beside the baby. "And what's this little one's name?"

"Mary. My cousin doesn't get up this way very often. Their sitter fell through at the last minute. They dropped the baby off on their way to Washington to a client dinner. They'll only be there for one night."

Dave continued his examination of the baby. "I've seen a lot of this virus in my office in the past few days, vomiting and high fever. Has she been able to keep anything down?" he asked.

"Only a little bit of spring water."

"How old is she?" he asked.

"Four months," Scottie said.

Dave glanced at his wife. "Did you bring in the bag of samples?" Anna removed a plastic bag from her purse, and handed it to him. He dumped an assortment of Motrin and Pedialyte on the coffee table. He filled a small applicator with orange liquid and inserted it in Mary's mouth. "Repeat this dosage every six hours if her fever persists. Feed her Pedialyte until the vomiting subsides, then ease her back into her formula.

"Be aware of the signs of dehydration." He began to tick each one off on his fingers as he spoke. "If she goes more than six hours without wetting a diaper. If her urine is dark and smells strong. If she doesn't produce tears when she cries. There are others, you can Google them, but those are the most prominent ones." Stuffing his instruments in his black doctor's bag, he stood to go. "I mean this, Scottie. Regardless of whether you have an insurance card for this baby or not, if you have any concerns about her health, take her to the hospital right away."

Scottie bit her lip. "I understand."

"Okay, then. Anna, I'll wait for you in the car."

Because of his gentle manner and special way with children, Dave was one of the most sought after pediatricians in the area. Anna and Dave met in Boston, when she was at Boston College and he in medical school at Harvard. They'd only been dating for six months when she brought him home to meet her family and friends. Scottie had liked Dave from the start.

Tonight, however, Dave's manner was brisk, professional but lacking his usual cheery disposition. When he refused to look Scottie in the eye and neglected to kiss her cheek on his way out, Scottie knew he suspected something amiss about the baby.

"Did you hear about the missing baby in the Monroe Park case?" Anna asked Scottie when the two of them were alone.

Scottie felt her best friend watching her, waiting for a

response. "Yes, I heard that. It's terrible," she mumbled, unable to meet her friend's eyes.

Anna wrapped her arms around Scottie and the baby. "You know you can call me anytime. But Dave . . . well, you understand. He can't risk losing his license."

11

M ary's fever broke within the hour but the vomiting and diarrhea persisted throughout the night and into the next morning. Sitting in the rocking chair in the nursery, Scottie had dozed off and on in between changing dirty diapers and soiled linens and keeping a watchful eye on the baby for dehydration.

Brad didn't come home at all, which was fine by Scottie. She didn't have the energy for an argument she could never win.

Anna texted once, right after she left, a message she was sure came straight from Dave's mouth: *You are playing a dangerous game, Scottie. If anyone asks, we were never there.*

Will texted off and on throughout the night, each text more pleading than the next. Any other time of year, her brother would have shown up at her door, but he was swamped at work with end-of-the-year finances.

At 8:15 pm: *If u r in some kind of trouble, I want to help.*

At 9:20 pm: *I'm still at the office but I can be there in minutes.*

At 10:38 pm: *Talk to me, Scott.*

At 10.44 pm: *I can't help you if I don't know what's wrong.*

At 12:15 am: *Answer me, damn it.*

Not wanting to involve Will anymore than was necessary, she decided to wait until Mary turned the corner before she responded. She needed his help, and she was prepared for him to bombard her with questions. She only hoped she could convince him he was better off not knowing the answers.

At six thirty, she turned on the television in her bedroom and scrolled through the local channels, relieved to find there'd been no further developments in the missing baby case during the night. The situation was out of her control. Scottie felt like a sitting duck, waiting for someone to take aim and fire at her.

The baby's vomiting subsided sometime around ten o'clock. Scottie planned to wait until noon before feeding the baby some formula. If everything went well, she would be on the road by two.

She bathed the baby, then showered and dressed in jeans and a warm wool sweater. She'd just finished eating a bowl of tomato bisque and was preparing Mary's bottle when Joyce Jackson led the noon news with yet another breaking story.

"I'm standing at the iron fountain in Monroe Park where an eyewitness has come forth with some pertinent information in the missing baby case." Joyce spread her arm out wide to the scene behind her where a group of bystanders were gathered around several police officers. "At least one eyewitness claims to have seen a woman in the park the morning the baby went missing. According to this source, the woman is no stranger to Monroe Park. Known to them as the camera lady, this woman visits with the homeless often, bringing with her hot food and provisions."

Scottie gasped. Her heart racing, she broke out in a cold sweat. She reached for the controller and turned the volume up.

"Do you have a description of this camera lady?" asked Sylvia Sheldon, the buffed and polished newscaster in the studio.

Joyce consulted her notes. "Attractive. Tall with blonde hair usually pulled back in a ponytail. Appears to be in her late twenties to early thirties."

"Have you received any information as to why the people of Monroe Park call her the camera lady?" Sylvia Sheldon asked.

Joyce shook her head. "Only that she likes to take pictures of them."

Scottie clicked off the television. She was so screwed. Anyone who had been in her house—not only her friends but repairmen and delivery people as well—had seen the photographs of the Five. This new development changed everything. Once the police identified Scottie, she'd become a wanted person. If she took the baby on the run, she'd never be able to come home to Richmond. She'd never see her family or friends again. If she turned herself in to the police, she could go to prison for kidnapping.

She knelt down in front of the baby, who was kicking her legs and swatting at the toys on her bouncy seat, playful for the first time in twenty-four hours.

"We'll just have to borrow more money from Will." She lifted Mary out of the bouncy seat and hugged her tight. "We need to get on the road as soon as you've got something in your tummy."

Forcing herself to take deep breaths, she sat down at the island and reached for her cell phone. She clicked on Will's contact information, but the call went directly to voice mail. A minute later, she received a text from him: *At lunch with important client. Will call you when done.*

Her phone dinged again with a text from Brad: *Keep me out of this, Scottie. I never saw that baby.*

"Fuck off, Brad," she screamed and threw her phone across the room. It bounced off the carpet and landed in front of the Christmas tree.

Scottie took several deep breaths, forcing herself to calm down. She figured she had at least a few hours before the police followed the bread crumbs to her front door.

Mary was finishing her bottle when the doorbell rang. Every hair on Scottie's body stood to attention. Placing the baby in the swing, she tiptoed to the front door and peeked through the peephole.

Logistically, there was no way her mother could have seen the noon news, unless she'd been watching with one of Scottie's neighbors. Will may have expressed his concern to their mother about the baby, but he was in a meeting. He didn't know the police had identified the camera lady as a possible suspect. With any luck, Barbara's timely appearance at her front door was merely a coincidence.

Scottie threw open the door. "Now is not a good time, Mother."

Barbara held up a scrawny-looking Fraser fir wreath. "I bought you a wreath, but I see you already got one. This one's pitiful looking anyway. It's the only one I could find." She tossed the wreath out into the yard and, brushing past Scottie, headed straight down the hall to the family room. "Whose baby is this?"

"She's mine, Mom. I found her." Even to herself, she sounded delusional.

"Oh, Scottie. What have you done?" The look of pity in her mother's face unleashed the torrent of emotion she'd been holding back.

"Oh God, Mom. I screwed up so badly." When Scottie burst into tears, the baby started to cry as well.

Barbara picked up the baby and jiggled her. "There, there, now. Everything will be okay," she said to the baby, but her eyes were on Scottie. She sank to the sofa and pulled Scottie down beside her. "Sit, honey, and tell me everything."

Eyeing her mother's St. John suit, Scottie handed Barbara a burp cloth. "She might spit up."

Barbara listened without interrupting as Scottie recounted her story from the discovery of the baby to the recent development broadcasted on the noon news. "I never intended to keep her, Mom. You've gotta believe me. All I could think about at the time was getting the baby to a warm house. I mean seriously, the poor thing was lying next to her dead mother. What else was I supposed to do?"

"Actually, the autopsy discovered that Melissa Sabin had an undetected genetic heart defect that caused her death."

Scottie jerked her head toward her mother. "Wait, what? How'd you know that?"

Barbara shrugged. "It was on one of the stations this morning."

So Melissa Sabin had a genetic heart defect. Does that mean Mary is at risk as well?

"How long have you known, Mom?"

"Your brother called me at daylight. I don't think he slept a wink worrying about you."

Scottie sighed. She couldn't very well be mad at her brother. After all, she was the one who'd ignored his texts. "That makes two of us. I was up all night with the baby. She has the stomach flu."

Instead of handing the baby back to Scottie—like she expected her mother to do in the event of possible contamination —Barbara held Mary even tighter. "The stomach flu is bad business. I hope you're feeling better now."

Aside from her fussy ways, Scottie knew her mother would make an excellent grandmother. Who knew what would become of the baby Scottie was carrying, if she even carried it to full term? It was not uncommon for grandparents to raise their grandchildren in today's world. But she couldn't imagine her parents raising her child while she was in prison anymore than she could see Brad as a single parent. Would she be forced to put the child up for adoption after all she'd been through to have a baby?

Scottie began to cry again, great wracking sobs that took her breath.

Barbara secured the baby in the swing and went to comfort her daughter. She wrapped her arms around Scottie and held her close. "We'll figure this out, honey. Don't you worry." She smoothed her hair and rubbed her back. "We'll get you the very best help money can buy."

When Scottie's sobs finally subsided, her mother held her at arm's length. "How does Brad feel about all this?"

"He doesn't approve of me keeping the baby."

"Finally something Brad and I agree on." Her mother fished her cell phone and a pocket-size pouch of tissues out of her bag. Handing the tissues to Scottie, she punched a number into her phone and held it to her ear.

"Who are you calling?" Scottie asked, blowing her nose.

"Your father, of course."

Scottie snatched the phone away from her mother. "You mean he doesn't already know?"

Barbara shook her head. "Will made me promise I wouldn't tell your father until I knew for sure what we were dealing with. We're in deep trouble here, sweetheart. We need your father to call in the troops."

12

For the next hour, Scottie begged and pleaded with her mother not to call her father. "Please, Mom. Just lend me some money. Give me my Christmas check early. Anything. I'll pay you back, I promise. Once I get settled in Canada."

"In Canada? Listen to yourself, Scottie. You're talking crazy."

"No I'm not. Except for the money part, I've got it all figured out. I'll drive up to New York tonight. Once I find someone to forge a fake passport for me and a birth certificate for Mary, we'll cross the border into Canada and disappear." Scottie dropped to her knees in front of her mother. "Don't you see, Mom? I can't give Mary up now. This is the only hope I have of keeping her."

"There must be another way. I'm sure your father's legal team can come up with something to get you out of this mess."

"They'll take the baby from me and lock me away at Tuckers. Or worse, send me to prison." Scottie got to her feet and dropped her mother's cell phone on the cushion beside Barbara. "If that's what you want for me, go ahead and call Dad." She lifted Mary out of the baby swing. "Before you do, though, you should know that I'm pregnant. Do you really want your grand-child born in prison?"

Barbara took in a sharp breath as her hand flew to her chest. "I'd say this complicates the situation."

"You think?" Scottie scooped up an armful of bottles and formula from the kitchen counter. "Since you're not willing to help me, I'm going upstairs to call Will."

Scottie locked herself in the nursery. She knew she was acting like a spoiled child threatening to run away if she didn't get her way. But she didn't care. Merry Mary was a part of her now. If she had to fight to keep her, so be it. She had nothing to lose. If they caught her, she was going to prison.

Her mother would call her father, regardless of what Scottie wanted. He would drop what he was doing and rush right over. She imagined the disappointment in his cornflower eyes that were so like her own. The concern for Scottie's well-being—her mental stability and the strong likelihood that his baby girl might go to prison—would be etched in the lines in his face.

Just as Will was a mama's boy, Scottie had always been her father's little princess. "His and her children," her parents always joked to one another. Whenever the family separated into groups of two—to go on rides at Disney World or play charades or take trips to tour colleges—Scottie always paired up with her father while Will went with their mother. Same was true in family arguments. Barbara always took Will's side and Stuart defended his daughter. Will went to Barbara with his problems, while Scottie sought advice from her father. Except, of course, for instances when she was facing prison time for kidnapping a child.

The baby's eyelids began to droop while Scottie was changing her diaper. "Time for you to go night-night, little one." She placed Mary in her crib and tucked the blanket around her. "When you wake up, after your feeding, we'll be on our way to our new life."

Scottie curled up in the rocking chair and called Will. He

answered on the second ring. "Thanks for telling Mom about the baby," she said in a low voice so as not to disturb Mary.

He let out a sigh. "You left me no choice. You would've done the same thing in my shoes, and you know it. I'm afraid for you, Scott."

Scottie twirled a curl around her finger. "I know. I'm not mad at you."

"Well I'm mad as hell at you. Why'd you do it, Scottie? You'll get your baby. Just not like this."

"You don't understand, Will."

"Then explain it to me."

"I had no intention of keeping the baby at first, not until Mabel came to visit me."

"Who's Mabel?"

"The oldest of the five homeless people I've been photographing in Monroe Park. She reminds me of May Belle. Remember her? Nana's old housekeeper who always made ice cream floats for us everytime we visited."

"Of course I remember May Belle. Stay focused here, sis. What does this Mabel person have to do with you deciding to keep the baby?"

"She helped me see that the baby is better off with me. What happened that day in Monroe Park is no different than what happened centuries ago in Bethlehem. Mary is a gift from God, Will. To me."

A long silence ensued before he responded, "Okay . . . so, I understand how you might actually believe this, considering the circumstances, but—"

"You don't even know all of the circumstances. There are no strings attached. According to Mabel, the baby's mother doesn't know who the father is. And there's no birth certificate because the baby was born in the park."

"Except that now Melissa Sabin's parents have shown up to identify the body of their dead daughter, a teenage runaway they've been looking for for five years. My guess is, the baby's grandparents will not give up on finding their missing grandchild. She's the only piece they have left of their daughter."

"Never mind that they are abusive alcoholics who nearly beat Melissa to death before she ran away."

"How do you know that?"

"Mabel told me."

"And you believe this woman without hearing both sides of the story. Since when do you trust a source without doing the research?"

A lone tear escaped Scottie's eye and rolled down her cheek. He was right. She'd wanted so much to believe Mabel, she'd turned a blind eye to all the other possible scenarios. At some point, probably in the very beginning, she'd stopped thinking with her head and started listening only to her heart.

"I agree that having the grandparents show up complicates things."

Scottie heard the frustration in her brother's voice when he said, "Look, Scottie, Dad is on his way over there with one of his attorneys. At least listen to what they have to say."

She began to cry in earnest now. "I'm pregnant, Will. I can't deliver this baby in prison."

"What? Jesus, Scottie!" He paused, breathing hard. "Just hold tight. I'll be there as soon as I can."

13

After thirty minutes of coaxing from her father, Scottie finally agreed to come out of the nursery and talk to his lawyer. But only on her terms. Stuart Westport reluctantly agreed to lend her money to start a new life if she didn't like what his lawyer had to say.

To Scottie's surprise, she found love and compassion and no trace of disappointment in her father's eyes.

They gathered in the dining room, around the mahogany double-pedestal table she'd inherited from her nana. Her mother served coffee in the cups and saucers Scottie had received as wedding gifts, part of the fine hand-painted china Barbara insisted every young bride should have. When they moved into the house, Scottie had stored the china set out of the way in the cabinet above the refrigerator. Had her mother been snooping through all of her things?

"I'll just be in the other room with the baby," Barbara said, and slipped quietly out of the room.

Her father reached across the table and squeezed Scottie's hand. "Mr. Bingham will take good care of you, honey. He's our best criminal attorney."

Her father had joined forces with his best friend right out of law school to create their own firm, Westport and Johnson. Their two-man operation had grown to nearly one hundred attorneys that covered nearly every area of law from corporate litigation to estate planning to divorce. They even employed several attorneys to handle criminal cases when one of their regular clients broke the law.

Scottie had met all of the attorneys at Westport and Johnson at some point over the years. She knew some of them better than others. With bright blue eyes behind wire-rimmed glasses perched atop his chubby pink cheeks, Len Bingham had a face she thought she could trust.

Although she suspected Bingham to be in his late fifties, he appeared much older than her father. Aside from a strip of hair around the base of his skull, he was mostly bald—and overweight by an easy fifty pounds. In contrast, her father was trim and fit with the healthy glow of an outdoorsman and a solid head of sandy-colored hair.

The attorney loosened his tie and rolled up his shirtsleeves, preparing to get his hands dirty. When she seemed hesitant to discuss her situation, he said, "Your father is paying me a retainer, Scottie. Regardless of what actions you decide to take, nothing you tell me will leave this room."

Mr. Bingham made notes on the legal pad in front of him while Scottie stammered through the events of the past few days. When she finished telling her story, he asked her a number of questions before discussing his observations. He presented the potential scenarios and listed the charges the police may decide to bring. They sat around the table for what seemed like hours, long after the coffee in Scottie's cup grew cold. All the what-ifs and maybes made her head spin, but the one thing he didn't offer was a way out.

Scottie clasped her hands in front of her. "Let me ask you

this, Mr. Bingham. How do the guards treat pregnant inmates in prison?"

Bingham cast a nervous glance at her father. "Are you telling me you're pregnant?"

Scottie rubbed her hand across her flat belly. "Six weeks if my calculations are correct."

"Did you know this at the time of the abduc . . . um, when you discovered the baby in the park?"

Scottie stood abruptly. "No, sir, I did not. And frankly, I don't see what difference it makes whether I was pregnant at the time or not. We've talked a lot about intent here today. My *intent* was to take the baby someplace warm and safe. Nothing more."

Bingham stood to face her. "I'm sorry. I didn't mean to offend you."

Scottie held her hand out to him. "I appreciate your time, Mr. Bingham, but I need to talk to my family before I make my decision."

Bingham ran his hand over the shiny dome of his head. "You realize you're taking a big risk. If the police receive evidence that leads them to you . . . well, let's just say you'll have better bargaining power if you go to them on your own volition instead of waiting for them to come to you."

"With all due respect, Mr. Bingham, I'm not convinced they'll come to me."

Bingham shot her father a look, a plea for him to intervene. Stuart shrugged. "I made a deal with my daughter. I convinced her to listen to you. Now she'll have to make up her own mind on how to proceed."

Bingham unrolled his sleeves and removed his suit jacket from the back of the chair. "I understand." He handed Scottie a business card with a long list of numbers and email addresses on it. "Call me anytime, night or day."

Scottie waited in the dining room while her father showed his partner to the door. "You heard him yourself, Daddy," she said when Stuart returned. "Your attorney thinks I'm guilty. He started to use the word abduction but caught himself. I don't stand a chance if I stay in Richmond. They'll trace my credit cards if I try to use them. Please, can you just loan me some money until I get settled?"

"Let's see what your mother has to say." Stuart wrapped an arm around Scottie's shoulder and ushered her into the family room where her mother was flipping through the December issue of *Virginia Living* magazine and sneaking peeks every few seconds at the baby lying on the sofa next to her.

"Scottie and I need to talk to you," Stuart said.

"Talk to me about what?" Barbara said, looking up from her magazine.

"About Scottie leaving town." Stuart faced his daughter, holding her at arm's length. "I'm not opposed to lending you the money, honey. I'm just worried you're making the wrong decision."

Her chin set in determination, Scottie said, "If you don't loan me the money, Dad, I'll find someone else who will."

"When are you planning to leave?" Barbara asked.

"A lot depends on what the police discovered today." Scottie retrieved the remote from the coffee table and clicked on the early edition news. A few minutes into the broadcast, Joyce Jackson announced that no further developments had taken place in the case of the missing baby.

Barbara's shoulders relaxed as the tension seemed to drain from her body. "So there's no urgency in you leaving."

Scottie shook her head. "Not necessarily. I still think it's best if we leave tonight, after I feed Mary her bedtime bottle. Traveling after dark gives us an advantage."

Stuart removed his wallet and counted six, crisp hundred-dollar bills out on the counter. "That's all I have in my wallet. If you wait until the morning, I can get more."

Scottie's mother emptied her wallet of five twenties. "You can't get far on seven hundred dollars, Scottie."

No kidding, Scottie thought. *The fake documents alone will cost more than a thousand bucks.*

"I'll borrow some from Will. You guys have already done enough, paying for the attorney and all." Scottie picked the baby up off the sofa. "I'm going upstairs to rest and wait for Will. He should be here any minute. You can see yourselves out, can't you?"

"Please don't do this, Scottie." Barbara's eyes filled with tears. "I beg you to stay. You can hide out at the farm until this all blows over."

"And make you guys accomplices? No way. Besides, they don't have hair stylists and nail technicians in prison." Scottie smiled at her mother, then hugged her tight, squeezing the baby between them. She turned to her father. "Or golf courses and duck blinds for you." She stood on her tiptoes and kissed his cheek.

Taking a step back from her parents, she tried to memorize their faces. Who knew when she'd see them again, if she'd see them again? They weren't getting any younger.

"Please don't worry about me. You taught me well. I'm a fighter."

14

From the nursery upstairs, Scottie heard her parents' muffled voices mixed in with sounds from the television in the family room beneath her. She thought she'd made it clear she wanted them to leave. Were they waiting for Will to arrive, the changing of the guard from the wardens to the night watchman, to make certain she didn't leave town?

Her phone vibrated in her pocket with a text from Brad: *Can you pack some clothes for me and leave the bag beside the front door?*

Did this mean he was leaving her, abandoning her in her moment of need?

She responded: *Whatever.*

Leaving Mary to play in her crib, she located another duffle bag at the back of her closet and crammed some of his clothes and his toiletries inside. Ignoring the blast of cold air that penetrated the room, she opened their bedroom window and dropped the duffle bag to the sidewalk below.

She gathered Mary in her arms and returned to the rocking chair. A few minutes later, the sound of her parents talking with Will in the foyer drifted up the stairs. She heard the front door close, followed by the pounding of feet on the stairs. Will appeared in the doorway of the nursery with a Chipotle bag in one hand and a pint of Jack Daniels in the other. "Whose duffle bag is that on your sidewalk?"

"Brad's. I guess he's leaving me."

"Fuck Brad." He held out his arms. "I brought provisions. Brain food for you, and brain booze for me. Let's go downstairs." He used his right elbow to wave her on. "We need to put our heads together and figure this thing out."

She dragged herself to her feet and followed him downstairs. "I don't know what makes you think you're smarter than the best criminal attorney in the city." She dropped to a barstool at the island. "If Len Bingham can't come up with a solution . . ."

"That's because he's trying to defend you." He removed the lid from her burrito bowl and placed it in front of her. "I'm trying to find a way out of your mistake." He poured bourbon over ice cubes in a tumbler.

"I made a colossal one this time for sure," she said in a voice loud enough to be heard over the Alka-Seltzer commercial on TV. She waved her hand at the television. "Will you please turn that thing down? Dad gets harder of hearing every day."

Will found the remote and turned the volume down.

With the baby sleeping peacefully in the crook of her arm, Scottie picked at her burrito bowl, and Will sipped on his bourbon, while they explored the situation from every angle imaginable. When they'd exhausted the topic, Scottie said, "See, I told you it's hopeless. I have no choice but to leave town."

"I'm not giving up that easily. There's gotta be something we're missing." Will drained the rest of his bourbon and sucked on a cube of ice while he contemplated her problem. When his eyes caught sight of something on the television, he scrambled for the remote.

He punched the volume up and Joyce Jackson's voice filled the room. "I'm here this evening with Judith and Michael Sabin, the parents of the young woman found dead in Monroe Park just six days ago."

Joyce was standing in front of a nondescript building, presumably downtown, with a young-looking, middle-aged couple. Scottie got up and went to stand in front of the television.

Abusive alcoholics? I don't think so.

Average in size and shape, with sad expressions, they appeared to be honest, hard-working Americans, perhaps a kindergarten teacher and an insurance salesman.

"Have there been any recent developments in the case of your missing granddaughter?" Joyce held the microphone out to Judith.

"The police have asked us not to comment on the case. We're here today to appeal to the person who has our grandchild, the mysterious camera lady. We've lost our only child, our runaway daughter who we haven't seen in years. Please, we beg you to give us a chance to know our grandbaby. She's all we have left of our family." Judith began to cry and Michael put his arm around her to comfort her.

The camera panned back to Joyce. "If you have any information regarding the whereabouts of the mysterious camera lady or the Sabins's missing grandchild, please contact the police immediately. That's all for now, Wally. Back to the studio."

Scottie dropped to the sofa. "Oh God, Will. What have I done?"

Her brother jumped to his feet and began pacing around the kitchen island. "Maybe . . . just maybe."

Scottie could almost see the wheels turning in his head. "Maybe what, already?"

He stopped pacing. "I've got an idea." His chocolate eyes bounced back and forth between Scottie and the baby in her arms. "But I'm not sure it'll work."

"Tell me, damn it."

He hesitated, a faraway look crossing his face, as though he was struggling with an inner conflict. "Let me ask you this. If you had a chance to give the baby back and walk away scot-free— pardon the pun— would you take it?"

Scottie looked at the baby in her arms, who stared back up at her with such adoration it made her heart do somersaults. Gripping her tighter, she kissed the top of Mary's head. "Honestly, I don't know," she said, letting out a deep breath.

Will came to sit beside her on the sofa. "Think about it, Scottie. Are you really the kind of person who would knowingly keep a baby from her biological family? If you are, then you're not the Scottie I know."

"A week ago, I never would have considered doing something so despicable, but now I'm not so sure. I've never experienced this kind of close bond before. I don't know how to describe it. I only know I can't walk away from her."

Somewhere along the way, she'd fallen for Mary. Even if she carried the baby in her womb to term, she would always have to share her or him with Brad. But Mary, she felt, belonged solely to her, her very own special someone.

"That's the thing, Scott. You're too close to the situation, too emotionally involved, to think objectively. Trust me when I tell you this is not the right choice for you. What kind of life will you have on the run, always having to look over your shoulder? You won't be able to hold a steady job or give Mary a proper education. And think about your baby. How will you pay for the medical bills? The police will be watching Mom and Dad, and me, which will make it difficult for us to send you money."

Scottie hadn't considered how her actions might affect her family. Aside from the public humiliation, they would be forced to live in their own prison, constantly watched by the police. She'd miss her parents, of course. Her mother's good cooking and her father's warm smile. Her mother's zest for life and her father's gentle ways. But a life without Will was unimaginable.

No more late-night gossip sessions over a large pepperoni pizza from Chanello's. No more spur-of-the-moment day trips to Virginia Beach. No more lingering Saturday lunches on the porch at The Continental. No more Christmas Eve dinners at their parents' farm or New Year's Eve parties at the Homestead. No, a life without Will would not do at all.

"What're you thinking, Will?"

He got to his feet. "Let me figure a few things out before I tell you." He slipped on his coat and turned to walk away.

"Wait a minute. Where are you going?" she asked following him to the front door.

"To find a solution to your problem." He opened the door.

"If you're not back by ten, I'm leaving, Will, one way or another."

He glanced at his watch. Seven fifteen. "I'll be back way before then. If not, I'll call you. Promise me, Scottie, whatever you do, don't leave until you hear from me." He kissed her cheek. "In the meantime, go eat your burrito bowl. You need to keep up your strength for both babies." He jabbed his index finger at her chest. "And think about what I said. I know Mary means a lot to you, but she will have a good life with her grandparents, and you have much to look forward to in yours."

15

S cottie felt too nauseous to eat. She placed Mary in the playpen, brewed a cup of tea, and curled up on the sofa.

While the baby dozed, she relived the events of the past six days, from the discovery of Melissa Sabin's dead body to her game-changing conversation with Will.

When she discovered the body, her primary goal, her only goal, had been to get the baby warm and fed and in the hands of someone who would protect her from a lifetime of abuse and neglect in the foster system. Mabel, with her tales of woe about Melissa's past home life, had cleared the way for Scottie's emotions, granting her permission to love the baby. And Scottie, an investigative journalist trained to search out the clues and scrutinize the facts, had never questioned one word.

She'd been prepared to vanish into the night with Mary, but her brother, always the sensible Will, had helped her see that her choices of late had been based on emotion rather than logic. She glanced over at the stack of hundred-dollar bills on the counter. Realistically, how far would seven hundred dollars get her? As a photographer or a journalist or as a combination of the two, she had talents to offer the world, skills that would, under normal circumstances, earn her a decent keep. But no one would hire her without a resume. All her hard work in high school, college, and beyond would be washed down the drain. She could very well end up delivering her baby in a park—just like Melissa Sabin had done.

While the baby slept, Scottie wandered around the house, admiring her shabby chic decor. She'd spent afternoons combing antique malls and yard sales searching for just the right walnut chest for the living room and mahogany sideboard for the dining room. She'd chosen the colors and painted all the rooms herself —soft grays downstairs with an accented wall of aqua in the kitchen, a cheerful yellow for the nursery and calming lavender for the master bedroom upstairs. The house itself deserved praise —the ten-foot ceilings and intricate woodwork around the fire-places, the random-width oak floors and handblown glass windowpanes.

Her father had given her the money for a down payment on the house, along with the stipulation that Scottie's name be the only one on the mortgage. She was, after all, the primary bread-winner. Brad had seemed fine with the arrangement, a little too much for Scottie's liking if truth be told. She thought she'd married a man who could pull his own weight but discovered, instead, she'd married a freeloader.

What would happen to the house if she left town? Brad would default on the loan and the bank would foreclose. All of her precious belongings would be sold at a yard sale.

She felt a jabbing pain in her chest, as though her heart was being torn into two pieces, with Mary on the one side, while on the other, the life she'd work so hard to create—her family, her career, the baby growing inside of her.

After hours of agonizing deliberation, Scottie had resigned herself to leaving town, and was feeding the baby her bedtime bottle when Will finally returned a few minutes before ten. He was wearing a huge grin and carrying a big brown shopping bag.

"What's this?" she asked, pulling out a wig with long brown dreadlocks and a trench coat streaked with dirt and grime.

"Your disguise."

"And where am I supposed to wear this disguise, in the car on my way out of town?"

"Not exactly what I had in mind." He handed her a folded slip of paper.

She opened the note. *Omni Room 365* was scrawled across the paper. She looked up at her brother. "I don't get it. Who's staying at the Omni?"

"Melissa Sabin's parents."

She looked at him, incredulous. "And you expect me to just waltz in there and hand Mary over to them."

"Not waltz, no. Hence the disguise. I've scouted out the place. It's nearly deserted. I guess no businessmen are traveling this close to Christmas."

"I don't know, Will. It sounds risky. What about security cameras?"

"I've got it all figured out, if you'll just listen to me." He sat down on the sofa next to her. "I truly believe this is your best chance to walk away from this situation."

She listened as he described his plan in detail. He'd considered everything, and responded to all her questions with reasonable answers. While his plan wasn't risk-free, she agreed it was her best chance, her only chance, to walk away.

"And what if I get caught?" Scottie asked.

"You'll text me a 911 message. I'll call Dad, who will contact his attorney, and the three of us will meet you at police headquarters. I'll make sure you don't go through this alone, sis. The judge is more likely to go lenient on you if you're caught trying to give the baby back rather than sneaking her out of town under the cloak of darkness."

"True." Scottie sat back on the sofa with the baby on her knees. "I guess this is it, little one, my Merry Mary. It's time for you to meet your nana Judith and granddaddy Michael."

16

S cottie stood in front of the mirror in her bedroom. She hardly recognized herself in dreadlocks, which was exactly the point. "I look like one of the Five. Where'd you get this stuff anyway?"

Will was standing next to her, holding the baby. "I wore the wig to a Halloween party several years back, but I bought the coat at Target. I drove over it a few times with my truck to get the tattered look." He flashed his naughty boy grin at her in the mirror. His eyes zeroed in on her bare feet. "What shoes are you gonna wear?"

"Boots, I guess." She walked over to her closet and dug through the dozens of pairs of shoes littering the floor. "I guess these will have to do." She tugged on a pair of Hunter wellies.

"I don't know many homeless people who wear designer boots, but I guess they'll have to do."

Scottie wrapped two ratty-looking scarves around her neck and the bottom part of her face. "I need to cover my eyes. Maybe I should wear my sunglasses."

She dug through her purse for her Ray-Bans. "What'd you think?" she asked, meeting Will's eyes in the mirror.

He shook his head. "Too preppy. Keep your head bent and you'll be fine."

Scottie tossed the sunglasses back into her bag.

"Are we ready?" he asked.

"I just need to pack some supplies for the baby," Scottie said, already on her way to the nursery. She gathered diapers, wipes, and two clean sleepers from the nursery, then went to the kitchen downstairs and stuffed them in a plastic grocery bag along with formula and bottles.

She took the baby from her brother. "Give me a minute, please, Will?" She walked the baby over to the Christmas tree. "We did a good job on the decorations, you and me. We made a good team." She planted a kiss on the baby's forehead. "I'll never forget you, Merry Mary. I will always be thinking about you—wondering about your first steps, your first tricycle, your first date." She held the baby high over her head, then brought her back down and twirled her around in circles. "You were never meant to be mine. I know that now. You've taught me so much and I've cherished every minute of my time with you." Tears filled her eyes, blurring her vision.

Will appeared at her side. "We need to get going, Scott."

She nodded, not trusting her voice to speak.

He wrapped his arm around her and ushered her to the door and down the sidewalk. Will switched the car seat to his truck and helped Scottie strap the baby in. They rode in silence through the side streets to downtown. He pulled into a deserted parking lot a block west of the Omni Hotel. Scottie got out of the truck, removed Mary from the car seat, and slipped her into the baby carrier she wore beneath her trench coat. Crawling back into the front seat of the truck, she carefully fastened the seat belt around the baby.

"Remember the signals?" Will asked.

"Yes. *All clear* means I'm ready for you to pick me up, and *911* means we've got trouble."

"Right." He parked the truck on the curb next to the side entrance. "I'm gonna park somewhere close by so I can get to you a hurry." He held his fist out to her. "You got this, right?"

She inhaled a deep breath. "I sure as hell hope so."

"You'll be fine. Keep your head tucked so no one can see your face, and whatever you do, don't lock eyes with anyone. The elevators are right inside the side entrance."

Scottie tossed the diaper bag over her shoulder and entered the empty lobby. Her eyes glued to the ground, she rode the elevator to the third floor and tapped lightly on the door of room 365. A woman Scottie recognized from television as Judith Sabin cracked opened the door but left the chain on. Her eyes grew wide with alarm at the sight of the bedraggled woman in front of her.

"I have information about your granddaughter," Scottie whispered.

Michael Sabin appeared behind his wife, cell phone in hand ready to call the police.

Scottie opened the trench coat enough for them to see the top of Mary's head. "I'm the camera lady. I have your grandchild."

"Oh my goodness," Judith said, immediately unlatching the chain and opening the door wide.

Scottie lifted the baby from the carrier and placed her in Judith's arms. "Her name is Mary. At least that's what I've been calling her. I don't think your daughter . . . Melissa . . . well, I don't think she ever named the baby. There's no birth certificate, at least not that I know of."

Judith cradled the baby in her arms, hugging her tight and covering her face with kisses, while Michael peered at Mary over his wife's shoulder. His face softened and a warm smile appeared on his lips. "She looks just like Melissa did as a baby." Raising his head, he looked directly into Scottie's eyes. "I don't understand. Why'd you wait so long to bring her to us?"

"It's a long story." Scottie gestured at one of two chairs in the corner of the room. "May I?"

"I don't think that's such a good idea," he said after scrutinizing her odd attire, from her designer boots to her Rastafarian wig.

He knew she was wearing a disguise, of course. If only she could reveal the real Scottie to the Sabins. She wanted so much to assure them that their granddaughter had been in the capable hands of an educated, intelligent woman.

"Please," Scottie said to Michael. "Just give me a chance to explain. If you still want to call the police afterward, I totally understand."

Judith lowered herself to the king-size bed opposite Scottie. "Come on, honey. We owe her this much, for keeping our granddaughter safe."

He nodded once. "You have ten minutes."

Scottie drew in a deep breath. "I'm the one who discovered your daughter's body. I'm so sorry for your loss."

Judith brought her fingers to her lips and tears welled up in Michael's eyes.

Scottie waited a minute for the Sabins to rein in their emotions. "It was never my intention to keep the baby," she said, then described the events of the past week in great detail. She told them about finding the baby cradled in her dead mother's arms, and her decision to take her to safety. "When the others deserted me, with no cell phone to call the police, all I could think about was getting the baby somewhere safe and into the right hands."

She described that first miserable night when Mary's tummy had a hard time adjusting to formula, and she told them about her visit from Mabel. "The old woman convinced me the baby was better off living with me. Your daughter had painted an unflattering picture of you to her friends, I'm sorry to say. I have no reason to believe it's true, now that I've met you in person."

"What did she say about us?" Michael asked.

"That her family was dysfunctional and the two of you abusive alcoholics."

Judith shook her head in dismay. "That's just not true. Melissa was our only child. We tried our best with her. Maybe we tried too hard. She couldn't abide our strict rules. Our home became a battlefield over missed curfews and her poor performance in school. Her friends were all the wrong sort—drinking and drugs and promiscuous behavior. She ran off four years ago with a boy we didn't approve of."

Scottie raised her eyebrows. "Maybe he's the baby's father?"

"That's not possible," Michael said. "The young man my wife is talking about died of a heroin overdose a year later in Los Angeles."

"That's horrible," Scottie said.

"Everything about that way of life is horrible," Judith said. "We've been looking for Melissa for a long time. We've come into contact with several bands of homeless people in the process."

"You still haven't answered my question," Michael said. "Why'd it take you so long to come forward?"

"I'll be honest with you. In the past six days, I've grown quite fond of your grandchild. It's an easy thing to do. You see, the past couple of years have been difficult for me." She told them about her miscarriage as well as the stillbirth of her baby last spring. "I'm not making excuses for my behavior. I was vulnerable. When Mabel convinced me I was the best person to raise her, I took advantage of the situation. Lord knows why I listened to an old woman who's been living on the streets for the past twenty years. Because I wanted it so much to be true, I guess."

Judith reached over and patted Scottie's hand. "The important thing is, you decided to give her back now."

"And you just expect us to let you walk away without punishment? You committed a crime." Michael said.

"I know it's too much to ask, after what I did." Scottie's hand rubbed her flat belly. "You see, I'm pregnant again. I found out a few days ago. I don't want my baby born in prison."

"Where's your husband in all this?" Michael asked, his eyes glued on the small engagement ring and wedding band on Scottie's left hand.

"He's not involved," Scottie said, shoving her hand in the pocket of her trench coat, mentally reprimanding herself for forgetting to take off her ring. "Despite our problems having a healthy baby, he is very much opposed to adoption. He was out of town visiting relatives when I discovered the baby. He came home on Friday and moved out the next day."

Biting back tears, Scottie took a deep breath to steady her voice. "Look, I understand if you need to turn me in to the police, but I want you to know I'm not a threat to you. Or to your granddaughter. I only want what's best for her."

Judith's eyes pleaded with her husband. "I understand why this young woman made the choices she did. The important thing is, she did the right thing in the end. Nothing good would come from turning her in. Turning her in would mean only that another baby would be raised without her mother."

"How do we explain the baby's sudden appearance?" he asked.

"Perhaps you could play up the human interest aspect of the story by calling a press conference in the morning," Scottie suggested. "Maybe offer Joyce Jackson the exclusive."

Michael lifted the baby from his wife's arms. He sniffed her skin and nuzzled her neck, then held her tight against his chest. "Whatever we decide to do, we'll protect you just as you protected our grandchild." He kissed the top of Mary's head. "I like the name you chose for her. I think we'll continue to call her Mary."

Scottie stood to leave. "The name Mary seems appropriate for a baby born in a makeshift shelter to a mother who loved her dearly."

17

S cottie texted Will—*Mission accomplished*—as soon as Michael Sabin closed his hotel room door behind her, separating Scottie from Mary forever. What she didn't say to her brother was how she felt, like all the life had gone out of her and she'd never be happy again.

She walked down the hall as fast as her clunky Hunter boots would let her. She rode the elevator to the lobby and exited the building through the same side door she'd come in. She looked one way then another before texting her brother the *all clear* message. He arrived on the curb less than a moment later. Scottie jumped into the truck and buckled herself in, waiting until they'd rounded the corner before yanking off the wig. Will reached over and gave her knee a squeeze, but he knew not to speak to her yet. She was far from ready to talk.

The tears burned at the back of her throat, but she didn't cry. She knew she'd made the right decision. She'd felt the warmth and kindness in the hotel room, the compassion and understanding. Judith and Michael were loving people who would offer Mary a proper home. The mistakes they'd made with Melissa would only make them better parents for Mary.

"I'd kill for a glass of wine right now," Scottie said, breaking the silence when the Omni was ten blocks behind them. "I don't really want to go home."

"I figured that." Will made a quick U-turn and parked alongside the curb in front of the Village Cafe. "Will you settle for a glass of milk and a piece of pecan pie?"

She nodded, not trusting her voice to speak. Her brother knew her so well.

They located a booth by the window and placed their order with the sullen waitress.

"What have you told Brad?" Will asked when the waitress was out of earshot.

"Nothing yet. He's at work." Leaning back in the booth, Scottie pulled out her cell phone. "I guess I need to tell him something, though. Before he turns me in himself." She texted Brad: *I gave the baby back. No strings attached, or so it seems. This doesn't change anything between you and me. You walked out on me when I needed you the most.*

Scottie didn't expect him to respond right away. If at all.

"I guess we need to update Mom and Dad," he said. While they waited for the waitress to bring their pie, they exchanged texts with their parents—Scottie with her father and Will with their mother.

They lingered over coffee until the cafe's two o'clock closing time. "I really don't feel like being alone, tonight," Scottie said on their way to her town house. "Will you stay with me?"

"As long as I get to pick the movie."

Scottie choked up when she saw the baby paraphernalia scattered about the family room. "This is so hard, Will. It's not fair."

"I know, Scott. And having all this stuff around isn't going to make it any easier." He helped her to the sofa, draped a blanket around her shoulders, and handed her the television remote. "Find a movie, something upbeat, while I pack everything up."

While Scottie scrolled through the holiday movies on On

Demand, Will gathered all the baby equipment and took it upstairs to store in the nursery.

"*It's a Wonderful Life* isn't exactly what I had in mind," Will said when he returned to the family room, his arms loaded with pillows and blankets.

"Sorry. A tearjerker seemed appropriate for a night like tonight," she said, but they both fell asleep before George Bailey could save his brother from drowning in the frozen pond.

Joyce Jackson's chipper voice woke them at six thirty. "I'm standing in front of the Omni Hotel in downtown Richmond where a stunning new development has taken place in the missing baby case."

Scottie and Will scrambled to sit. Rubbing the sleep from her eyes, Scottie saw baby Mary cradled in Judith's arms.

"I'm here with Judith and Michael Sabin, the parents of Melissa Sabin whose body was discovered in Monroe Park last Thursday." Joyce held her microphone in front of the Sabins. "I understand you had a visitor during the night?"

Michael Sabin nodded. "My wife and I feel so blessed this Christmas Eve morning to have our grandchild back with us, where she belongs."

"Can you tell us about the events of the night that led to the baby's return?"

"I'm not at liberty to discuss the details, only to say that my wife and I are eternally grateful for the young woman for taking such good care of our grandchild in the days following our daughter's death."

"So you've reported the incident to the police?" Joyce asked.

"There's not much to report. The woman was dressed in disguise. Her identity remains a mystery. I'm convinced she never intended any harm to the baby, but was merely taking care of her until our daughter's body was identified and the family notified."

"Can you—" Joyce started, but Michael held his hand up to silence her.

"That's all I'm prepared to comment on for now. We have a plane to catch. We are taking our granddaughter home for Christmas."

Scottie fell back against the cushions. "Do you think they actually talked to the police?"

Will shrugged. "Hard to say from his vague answer, but I can't see the Sabins leaving town before talking to the police."

Her eyes traveled the room before landing on the Christmas tree, so bright and cheerful in contrast to the heaviness she felt in her heart. "What are we supposed to do, sit around here all day and wait for the police to show up?"

"Hell no." Will got up and pulled Scottie to her feet. "Go pack a bag. We're going out to the farm a day early. We can take the four-wheelers out, and spend some time with the horses. And I'm sure Mom could use our help getting ready for the party tomorrow tonight."

"Don't you have to work?" she asked.

"I have a few phone calls I need to make. Nothing I can't handle from the farm."

"You go on without me." She pushed him away. "I'm not much in the mood for Christmas."

"No one expects you to be in a good mood. Besides, it'll do you good to have a change of scenery." His eyes drifted to the ten-day forecast flashing across the screen. He pointed at the television. "Looks like more snow. We can make a snowman or have a snowball fight or sit by the fire all afternoon drinking hot"—he glanced down at her belly—"chocolate and watching movies."

"See, I'm no fun to be with right now. I can't even drink hot toddies. Ask one of your friends to go with you. What about that girl you took out the other night, the one who works at the Apple Store?"

"That didn't work out so well. Turns out she's smarter than me." Taking her hand, Will dragged Scottie down the hall to the stairs. "We've never spent a Christmas Eve apart. Of course, it won't be as much fun this year without Brad around to make fun of . . ."

When he tried to push her up the stairs, she grabbed hold of the railing, refusing to budge. "Speaking of Brad, I should probably stay here in case he comes home."

"That is one thing you most definitely should *not* do." They locked eyes in a battle of wills. When she looked away, he turned her chin back toward him. "Remember that Christmas Eve when Buddy got run over by the car?"

Scottie bit her lip, holding back the tears. "He almost died that night."

"Right. Remember how hard we prayed for a miracle?"

Scottie remembered. "We spent the night beside him on the floor in front of the fire. When we woke up the next morning, he was wagging his tail and licking our faces."

"We got our miracle that night. Old Buddy lived five more years after that."

Scottie smiled. They had loved that yellow Labrador retriever more than any pet they'd ever owned. And they'd owned a lot of them over the years, living on a farm.

"That's the thing, Scott. Miracles come in all shapes and sizes. You were Mary's miracle, not the other way around. She was blessed to have you take care of her in her time of need. But the baby growing inside of you is *your* Christmas miracle, your gift from God."

Scottie placed a protective hand on her belly. She was grateful to Will for his wise insights. Regardless of how Brad fit into her future, the baby she carried would forever be a part of her, her own flesh and blood that no one could ever take away.

ABOUT THE AUTHOR

Ashley writes books about women for women. Her characters are mothers, daughters, sisters, and wives facing real-life issues. Her goal is to keep you turning the pages until the wee hours of the morning. If her story stays with you long after you've read the last word, then she's done her job.

Ashley is a wife and mother of two young adult children. She grew up in the salty marshes of South Carolina, but now lives in Richmond, Virginia, a city she loves for its history and traditions.

Ashley loves to hear from her readers. Feel free to visit her website or shoot her an email. For more information about upcoming releases, don't forget to sign up for her newsletter at ashleyfarley.net/newsletter-signup/. Your subscription will grant you exclusive content, sneak previews, and special giveaways.

ashleyfarley.net
ashleyhfarley@gmail.com

44043576R00061

Made in the USA
Middletown, DE
02 May 2019